The Space Between The Mirror

Johnny Gee

Published by Golden Ember Edition, 2024.

This is a work of fiction. Similarities to real people, places, or events are entirely coincidental.

THE SPACE BETWEEN THE MIRROR

First edition. October 5, 2024.

Copyright © 2024 Johnny Gee.

ISBN: 979-8224108244

Written by Johnny Gee.

Table of Contents

Chapter 1: The Allure of the Mirror 1
Chapter 2: The First Glimpse of the Unfathomable 5
Chapter 3: Dreams of Forgotten Dimensions 10
Chapter 4: The Lure of the Abyss 14
Chapter 5: The First Doppelgänger 19
Chapter 6: Escaping the Mirror World 23
Chapter 7: Nightmares and Paranoia 28
Chapter 8: First Reflection 33
Chapter 9: The First Trap 38
Chapter 10: The First Trap Tightens 43
Chapter 11: Time and Memory Distortion 49
Chapter 12: Encountering the Eyeless Figures 54
Chapter 13: Psychological Breakdown 59
Chapter 14: Through the Shattered Glass 64
Chapter 15: The Reflection's Revenge 70
Chapter 16: The Last Door 76
Chapter 17: Haunted by Reflections 81
Chapter 18: Into the Dark Corners 86
Chapter 19: The Revelation of Shadows 92
Chapter 20: A World of Mirrors 98
Chapter 21: A Fragile Peace 104
Chapter 22: The Deepening Shadows 110
Chapter 23: The Thin Veil 115
Chapter 24: The Crossing 120
Chapter 25: The Return of the Light 126
Chapter 26: The Other Side 131
Chapter 27: The Echoes of the Past 136
Chapter 28: The Unveiling 141
Chapter 29: Beneath the Surface 146

Chapter 30: The Weight of Tomorrow 151
Chapter 31: A Door Left Open...157
Chapter 32: The Breaking of the Glass 163
Chapter 33: The Path of Wholeness....................................169
Chapter 34: The Final Pieces 173
Chapter 35: The Quiet Echo...178
Chapter 36: The Crack in the Glass 183
Chapter 37: The Space Between...188
Chapter 38: Echoes of the Mirror...192
Chapter 39: The Last Reflection 196
Chapter 40: The Door Closed 201

Chapter 1: The Allure of the Mirror

The day I found the mirror was like any other, the sun bleeding its last light over the distant hills, casting long shadows over the forgotten little shop tucked away on a nameless street. I wandered in, drawn more by boredom than by interest, not knowing that this small act of curiosity would open a doorway to horrors I had never imagined.

The shop was filled with the usual relics of bygone eras: dusty books, tarnished silverware, and peculiar artifacts that had long been forgotten by their original owners. But it was the mirror that caught my eye, standing in the corner like an ancient sentinel waiting for someone to notice it.

It was large, taller than I was, framed in dark wood that had warped with age. Intricate carvings, the likes of which I had never seen, wound their way around the frame. Twisting, almost writhing, they seemed to depict strange, inhuman figures—grotesque faces hidden among the curves and spirals, their eyes following me as I approached. The glass itself was dark, not the clear, bright reflection one might expect. It seemed almost to absorb the light, offering a faint, distorted reflection of the shop and the room behind me.

I stood there, staring into it, feeling an odd pull deep within my chest. The air around me grew thick, and for a moment, I could swear the glass rippled, like a surface disturbed by something lurking beneath it. I blinked, my breath caught in my throat, and in that moment of hesitation, I felt a coldness creep through me—a sense that I was being watched. I could feel it then, a presence behind the glass, though nothing but my own warped reflection stared back at me.

The shopkeeper, an old man with eyes that looked as if they had seen far too much, shuffled over. He cleared his throat, startling me from my trance.

"Ah," he murmured, his voice barely more than a whisper, "you've found it."

I tore my gaze from the mirror, suddenly feeling foolish. "Found what?"

"The mirror," he said, his eyes narrowing. "It's an old thing. Older than the shop itself, I'd reckon. Came from somewhere far away. Its origins... well, some things are better left unknown."

I glanced back at the glass, the warped reflection of myself still staring back, my features elongated, twisted in ways that defied reason.

"How much?" I asked, the words slipping from my mouth before I realized it. I didn't want the mirror—not really. But something inside me needed to possess it, to understand what it was hiding.

The old man's expression shifted, a shadow crossing his face. "Take it," he said, his voice suddenly hoarse. "No charge. Just... take it."

I hesitated. "What do you mean?"

His eyes darted toward the door, as though he wanted to be rid of me. "I can't keep it here any longer. It's been... causing problems. The dreams. The... shadows." He glanced nervously at the mirror, his voice dropping to a near-whisper. "It's yours, if you want it. Just get it out of here."

I should have left. I should have walked away, ignoring the strange pull of the mirror and the cold dread that was starting to pool in the pit of my stomach. But I didn't. Instead, I nodded.

"I'll take it."

The old man barely looked at me as he handed me a receipt, scribbling down the details in a hurry. He refused to touch the mirror, instead leaving me to arrange for it to be delivered to my home the following day.

That night, as I lay in bed, I couldn't shake the feeling that something had followed me home. The air in my room felt thick, stifling, as though the very atmosphere had become laden with a presence I couldn't see. When I closed my eyes, I dreamt of dark waters, of shifting shapes beneath the surface, of glass breaking and splintering into infinity.

In my dreams, I stood before the mirror again, but this time, the glass was no longer a mere reflection of the world around me. It had become a window, a doorway. And through it, I could see… **things**—things that shouldn't exist, things that crawled and writhed, creatures with too many limbs and faces that melted and reformed like shadows in the water.

I awoke in a cold sweat, my heart racing, the remnants of the dream clinging to me like a fog. The room was silent, but the oppressive weight of the dream lingered. For the first time in years, I felt truly afraid.

The mirror arrived the next day, delivered by two men who seemed eager to leave it behind as quickly as possible. I had them place it in the study, a small, dim room at the back of the house where I kept old books and trinkets. As they carried it in, I caught sight of my reflection again, but something about it seemed off—slightly distorted, almost imperceptibly wrong. But before I could inspect it further, the men hurried out, leaving me alone with the mirror.

Alone with **it**.

For the rest of the day, I avoided the study, finding excuses to keep myself busy elsewhere. But no matter what I did, I couldn't shake the feeling that something was **waiting**. The house felt different now, as though the presence of the mirror had somehow altered the very air around it. The shadows seemed deeper, the silence heavier. And in the corners of my vision, I thought I saw movements—**flickers of darkness** that disappeared when I turned to look.

Night fell, and the sense of unease only deepened. I found myself drawn to the study, despite the gnawing fear in my chest. I stood in front of the mirror, staring into it, waiting for something to happen.

For a long moment, nothing did. The reflection stared back, warped and twisted, but otherwise still.

Then, just as I was about to turn away, I saw it. A flicker. A movement just behind me, in the glass. I spun around, heart pounding, but the room was empty. I turned back to the mirror, and there, in the reflection, I saw something move again.

A shadow, dark and **hungry**, slipping through the glass.

It was waiting for me. Watching.

And I knew, deep down, that whatever it was... it would not leave me alone.

Chapter 2: The First Glimpse of the Unfathomable

That night, after the mirror was placed in the study, I lay in bed, staring at the ceiling, my mind swirling with the events of the day. There was something about that mirror—something wrong. I had been unable to focus on anything since its arrival. The image of my reflection, distorted and alien, clung to my thoughts like a parasite. The room around me, though silent and familiar, seemed less safe, as if something had shifted subtly in the fabric of reality.

I couldn't sleep. Not with the weight of that thing in my house, lurking just beyond my sight. An inexplicable dread crept up my spine, cold and insistent. I found myself listening intently to the silence, expecting—no, dreading—some noise, some movement from beyond my room.

Eventually, I could stand it no longer. I needed to see it again.

I rose from bed and padded down the hallway. The house was quiet, save for the soft creak of floorboards beneath my feet. My skin prickled as I neared the study. It felt as though the air had thickened, grown colder. The shadows along the hallway seemed longer, darker than usual, but I dismissed it as the effect of the moonlight filtering through the windows. Still, there was something about them, about their unnatural depth and stillness, that made me want to look away.

When I reached the door to the study, I hesitated. My hand hovered over the knob, trembling slightly. The silence behind the door seemed profound, as though the very space beyond had been emptied of sound, of life. And yet, I felt it again—the presence, the weight of unseen eyes pressing against me.

I opened the door.

The room was dark, save for a thin strip of moonlight that filtered through the small window, illuminating the outline of the mirror where it stood against the far wall. My heart pounded in my chest as I stepped inside, my eyes locked on the glass.

There was no reflection. No image of the room, no shadow of myself. Just darkness. A black void that seemed to devour the light around it. I froze, unable to tear my gaze away.

Then it happened.

The surface of the mirror **shifted**, rippling like water disturbed by an unseen force. At first, the change was subtle, a faint quiver that sent a wave of nausea rolling through my stomach. But then, the ripple grew stronger, and the darkness within the mirror began to churn, twisting and warping like a living thing. Shapes began to emerge from the depths—vague, distorted forms that defied reason, their outlines shifting and melding together like smoke.

I stepped back, my breath catching in my throat.

There, within the mirror, I saw **something**. It was no longer just a reflection, no longer just a glass surface reflecting my world. It had become something far worse—a window to another place, another reality.

And in that place, **they moved**.

At first, I could not comprehend what I was seeing. The forms in the mirror shifted too quickly, blurring and elongating in ways that made my eyes burn to watch. They were not human. Their shapes, though vaguely recognizable as figures, defied all natural laws—limbs that bent in ways that should not have been possible, faces that stretched and twisted in maddening contortions, too many eyes and mouths set in unnatural places. Their movements were fluid and unnatural, like shadows unmoored from the ground.

I felt an overwhelming sense of wrongness. These creatures, these things, should not exist. Their very presence was an affront to reality, and as I watched, a creeping horror began to take root in my mind. They were **aware of me**. I could feel it, the weight of their attention pressing through the glass like an oppressive fog, their formless eyes locked onto me.

I took another step back, but my legs felt weak, unsteady. My mind reeled, unable to process the nightmare before me. My reflection, or what remained of it, had begun to melt into the darkness, consumed by the things beyond the mirror. I couldn't move, frozen by the sheer enormity of the unknown before me.

One of the creatures—a towering thing with limbs like elongated shadows and a face that seemed to ripple and melt like wax—pressed against the glass. Its many eyes locked onto mine, each one glistening with a malevolent intelligence that sent icy tendrils of fear creeping through my veins. Its movements were slow, deliberate, as though testing the boundaries of the mirror, seeking a way through.

And then... the glass **cracked**.

It was faint, almost imperceptible, but I heard it. A hairline fracture formed at the very edge of the mirror, spreading like a web across the surface. My breath caught in my throat as I watched the crack slowly expand, each new line sending a fresh wave of dread coursing through me.

I took a shaky step forward, as though drawn by some unseen force, my eyes fixed on the crack. Something inside me screamed to run, to turn away and never look back, but my body refused to obey. The mirror pulsed with a strange energy, an insidious rhythm that seemed to echo deep within my chest, pulling me closer, closer...

And then I saw it.

Amidst the churning darkness, through the cracks in the glass, I caught a glimpse of something far worse than the creatures. It was **the place** beyond the mirror. It was vast, endless, a landscape of alien architecture and impossible geometry, its twisted structures bathed in a dim, sickly light that seemed to bleed from the sky itself. There were shapes there—massive, towering things that moved with a slow, deliberate grace, their forms too vast and incomprehensible to fully grasp.

This was no mere reflection. This was another world, a dimension that should never have been glimpsed by human eyes. A realm where the rules of nature held no sway, where reality itself was malleable, twisted into forms that defied reason. I felt an overwhelming urge to scream, but no sound escaped my lips.

I staggered back, my heart pounding in my chest, the crack in the glass spreading like a spider's web, threatening to shatter the fragile boundary between worlds.

I slammed the door shut, breathing hard, my mind reeling with the horror of what I had just witnessed. I stumbled back down the hall, nearly tripping over my own feet in my haste to put as much distance between myself and the mirror as possible.

But even as I fled, I knew. I could feel it.
The crack in the mirror was just the beginning.

Chapter 3: Dreams of Forgotten Dimensions

Sleep did not come easily after what I had witnessed. When it did finally claim me, it was not the peaceful oblivion I craved, but a swirling vortex of terror that plunged me deeper into the nightmare I had only begun to glimpse. It was as though closing my eyes had opened some ancient gate, and through it, the things I had seen beyond the mirror crawled into my mind.

The dream began as a descent, a slow spiral through a realm of darkness that seemed to stretch on for eternity. I was falling—not through space, but through **time**, through layers of forgotten realities. As I tumbled, I saw flashes of impossible worlds, glimpses of dimensions long abandoned by the forces that had created them. They were ancient, older than the stars, older than the very concept of time.

I fell past cities built on impossible angles, their towering structures bending in ways that defied logic, the skies above them burning with alien colors. These were not human places; they had never been touched by mortal hands. The air itself felt hostile, thick with the weight of eons, filled with whispers that gnawed at the edges of my consciousness.

And always, there were the **shadows**—twisting shapes that flitted through the corners of my vision, never fully seen but always present. They followed me through each world, each dimension, their forms warping and shifting with every blink of my eye. The closer I came to understanding them, the less sense they made. Some had too many limbs, some too few, and their faces—if they could be called faces—shifted and melted as though they existed in multiple realities at once.

The dream was suffocating, oppressive. I felt as though I was being pulled deeper and deeper into some dark, infinite void from which there was no escape. Each breath felt heavier, as if the air itself had turned against me, growing thicker and more poisonous the further I fell. I wanted to wake, to claw my way back to the surface of reality, but I could not. Something held me fast, pulling me down, down, into the very heart of the nightmare.

At last, I reached the bottom, or what I thought was the bottom. There, in the heart of that forgotten dimension, stood the **mirror**.

It was the same mirror from my study, yet larger now—towering above me like a monolith of dark glass. Its surface was smooth, but beneath that stillness, I could sense something terrible shifting, waiting. The reflections it cast were wrong, not mere imitations of what stood before it but distorted versions, twisted mockeries of reality.

I approached the mirror, though every instinct screamed at me to turn back, to flee. But there was nowhere to go. The world around me had dissolved into nothing, leaving only the mirror, a singular point of terrible focus in an infinite void.

As I drew closer, the glass rippled again, just as it had in the waking world. But this time, it was more pronounced, more violent, as though the things beyond were straining to break through. And then, through the ripples, I saw **them**.

They were the same beings I had glimpsed before, the same **cosmic horrors** that lurked beyond the veil of reality. Their forms were grotesque, their limbs too long, their bodies too thin, but it was their **eyes** that held me transfixed. Eyes that shone with an ancient, malevolent intelligence, as though they had been watching me for longer than I could comprehend. Watching, waiting, hungering.

Suddenly, the mirror cracked again, just as it had when I had stood before it in the study. But this time, the crack spread further, faster, splintering across the entire surface in jagged, terrible lines. Through the cracks, I could see the vastness of the place beyond—a **forgotten realm**, a world of shifting geometry and crumbling civilizations, bathed in a pale, sickly light that seemed to flicker and pulse with a life of its own.

I felt myself drawn toward the mirror, pulled by some unseen force, as though the beings beyond were calling me, inviting me into their world. The surface of the glass shimmered, and I could see my reflection again—warped, twisted, barely recognizable as human.

And then... **it smiled**.

That was when I woke, my body drenched in sweat, my heart pounding in my chest. I sat up in bed, gasping for breath, the weight of the nightmare still pressing down on me. My hands trembled as I wiped the sweat from my forehead, my mind reeling from the images that lingered in the corners of my vision.

For a moment, I thought I had woken to some semblance of normalcy, that I had escaped the horrors of the dream. But as I looked around the room, I felt the cold grip of terror tighten around my chest.

The shadows in my bedroom were deeper than they should have been, darker, as though the night itself had thickened and grown malicious. The air felt wrong, heavy, as though it was pushing down on me. And in the far corner of the room, just barely visible in the moonlight, I saw it.

A **shape**.

It was barely there, a shadow among shadows, but it was watching. I could feel its eyes on me, even though it had none.

I blinked, and it was gone.

But I knew, even then, that it had not truly left. It was waiting, biding its time, lingering just beyond the edges of reality. Watching. Always watching.

I did not sleep again that night.

Chapter 4: The Lure of the Abyss

I awoke the next morning to a dim, overcast sky and a pounding headache. My body was heavy, as though I had not rested at all. The remnants of the dream still clung to me, lingering in the back of my mind like a shadow I could not shake. There was no mistaking what I had seen. The things that lurked beyond the mirror, the vastness of the world they inhabited, the ancient, unknowable terror—it was all too vivid, too real to dismiss as mere fantasy.

I could not ignore it any longer. Something had followed me back.

The house was eerily silent as I made my way down the hallway, my steps slow and cautious. Every creak of the floorboards, every soft gust of wind outside the windows, seemed magnified in the oppressive quiet. My eyes flicked to every reflective surface I passed, expecting to see something there—a shadow, a movement just out of the corner of my vision—but there was nothing.

Not yet.

When I reached the door to the study, I hesitated again. The door stood closed, as I had left it the night before, but the air around it felt different. It was colder here, as though the very space around the study had been touched by something from beyond. My breath hitched in my throat as I reached for the doorknob, my hand trembling slightly.

The door creaked open, revealing the dimly lit room beyond. The mirror stood where it had the day before, but the air around it felt thicker, more oppressive, as though the atmosphere had been charged with some unseen force. The window let in only the faintest sliver of light, casting long, twisted shadows across the floor. The mirror's surface seemed darker, more solid, as if it were not merely reflecting the room, but swallowing it.

I stepped into the room, feeling that strange pull again, the same one that had gripped me the first time I had seen the mirror. It was as if something within the glass was calling to me, beckoning me closer, luring me toward the unknown depths that lay beyond.

I approached slowly, my heart pounding in my chest. The reflection in the mirror was faint, almost nonexistent. The room behind me seemed dim and distant, its details warped and obscured by the strange, dark surface of the glass. But there was more. As I stood before the mirror, I saw movement—just at the edge of the reflection. A flicker, like a shadow passing swiftly across the surface, so quick that I could almost convince myself it hadn't happened.

But I knew better now.

I took another step forward, close enough to see my own face in the reflection. It looked wrong, though I couldn't immediately place why. My features seemed stretched, elongated, my skin paler than it should have been. The eyes staring back at me were not quite my own—darker, colder, and filled with something... else. Some awareness that had not been there before. A presence that lurked behind my own gaze, watching, waiting.

I reached out, my fingers trembling as they brushed against the cold surface of the mirror.

The glass rippled.

Not like water, but like something **alive**. The surface of the mirror twisted and shifted beneath my touch, as though the boundaries between our world and whatever lay beyond were bending, straining to hold back whatever lurked on the other side.

And then I saw it.

A figure—dim at first, but growing clearer with every passing second—began to take shape behind the glass. It was tall, impossibly tall, its body thin and angular, with limbs that bent at unnatural angles. Its face—or what passed for a face—was featureless, a smooth, pale mask of skin with no eyes, no mouth. And yet, I could feel it watching me. I could feel its gaze piercing through the glass, cold and unblinking.

I froze, my hand still pressed against the mirror, my breath catching in my throat. The figure did not move, but its presence filled the room, pressing down on me like a weight I could not escape. Its formless gaze bore into me, searching, probing, as though it could see not only my physical body but the very core of my being.

And then, slowly, it began to move.

Its limbs bent and twisted as it stepped forward, crossing the impossible distance between us with a sickening fluidity that made my stomach churn. The glass did not impede it. The surface of the mirror rippled as it moved through, as though it were nothing more than a thin membrane separating our two realities. I staggered back, my heart hammering in my chest, my mind screaming at me to flee, to turn away, but I couldn't. I was rooted to the spot, paralyzed by the sheer impossibility of what I was witnessing.

THE SPACE BETWEEN THE MIRROR 17

The figure reached the edge of the mirror, its pale, featureless face inches from my own. Its presence was overwhelming, a crushing sense of wrongness that filled the air, making it impossible to breathe.

And then it **stopped**.

For a moment, time seemed to freeze. The figure stood there, half within the mirror, half in my world, its faceless head tilted slightly as though studying me. It was waiting.

I didn't know how long we stood there, locked in that terrible silence. Seconds? Minutes? Hours? It felt like an eternity. And then, without warning, the figure withdrew, its body melting back into the glass with the same sickening fluidity. The surface of the mirror rippled, and once again, I was left staring at my own reflection.

But something was different now. The cold dread that had filled the room before was still there, but it had changed. The figure had not left. I could feel its presence still, lurking just beyond the glass, watching me, waiting for the next opportunity to cross into my world.

I stumbled back, my legs weak beneath me, and fled the study, slamming the door shut behind me. My breath came in ragged gasps as I leaned against the wall, trying to calm the wild beating of my heart.

I had felt its presence before. In the dream. In the shadow that had watched me from the corner of my room the night before. But now... now it was real.

And I knew, with a sickening certainty, that it would not stop.

The mirror had opened a doorway. A doorway to something vast, something ancient, something I could not begin to understand. And now that it had seen me, now that it had touched my world, it would never let me go.

Chapter 5: The First Doppelgänger

The days that followed were a blur of dread and sleeplessness. The house had taken on a strange quality, as if it too were aware of the presence that now lurked just beyond the boundaries of my perception. The familiar creaks and groans of the old wood were now filled with ominous intent, and the corners of rooms seemed darker, as though shadows had become thicker, heavier. It felt as if the very walls were closing in on me, inch by inch, suffocating me beneath the weight of the unknown.

But it was the mirror, always the mirror, that consumed my thoughts.

I avoided it as best I could, but no matter where I went in the house, I could feel its pull. It was like gravity, dragging me back toward that dark surface, toward the **things** that waited within. I knew I should have removed it—should have shattered it, should have thrown it out—but the thought of doing so filled me with an irrational fear. What would happen if I broke the mirror? What would be released into my world? What was already creeping through the cracks?

I could no longer tell if I was awake or dreaming. My nights were filled with visions—terrifying glimpses of the alien world I had seen through the mirror. Strange landscapes, grotesque figures, and whispering voices that spoke in a language I could not understand. Always, always, they watched me. And always, there was **something else**, something worse that lurked just out of sight, waiting for the moment to step through.

One night, after hours of tossing and turning in bed, I gave in to the mirror's pull. The house was silent, the moonlight barely penetrating the thick curtains. I rose from bed, feeling as though I were in a trance, and made my way down the hall to the study. My hands shook as I pushed the door open, and the now-familiar oppressive cold greeted me like an old, malevolent friend.

The mirror stood before me, its dark surface gleaming faintly in the pale light. The air in the room felt thick, suffocating, as if it were being consumed by some unseen force. I knew I should have turned back, but I couldn't. The mirror called to me, the silent voice in my mind urging me forward.

I took a step toward it. Then another. My reflection appeared in the glass—warped, as always, but still recognizably me. And yet, there was something **off** about it. The figure in the mirror stood still while I moved closer, its eyes locked onto mine, unblinking, watching with a strange intensity that sent a chill down my spine.

I stopped just inches from the glass, my breath fogging up the surface. The reflection stared back, unmoving, its expression unchanged. But there was something about those eyes—something that felt wrong, alien. They weren't mine. They were **its**.

Then, without warning, the reflection **smiled**.

It was a slow, unnatural smile, twisting up one side of its face in a grotesque imitation of a human expression. My blood turned to ice. I hadn't moved—hadn't smiled—yet the reflection grinned at me, its eyes glinting with a dark, malevolent intent. I stumbled back, my heart racing, but the reflection remained where it was, still smiling, still watching.

And then it moved.

Slowly, deliberately, the reflection raised its hand and pressed it against the glass. I watched in horror as the surface of the mirror rippled beneath its touch, bending inward like a membrane, as though the figure were pressing against the boundary between worlds, trying to break through.

I couldn't move. My legs felt like lead, my body frozen in place by the sheer terror of what was happening. The reflection—no, the **thing** in the mirror—began to push harder, its hand sinking into the glass. I could see the lines of its palm, the curve of its fingers, all too real, all too human. But I knew—**I knew**—that it was not human. It was something else, something that had been watching me for far longer than I could comprehend.

With a sudden, sickening lurch, the figure's hand broke through the surface of the mirror.

I gasped, stumbling back further, my heart hammering in my chest as the hand reached toward me, impossibly long fingers curling in the air. The reflection's face twisted into a grotesque grin, its eyes gleaming with malicious intent. It was **pulling itself through**, inch by inch, its body slipping through the glass like water, its limbs distorting and stretching as it crossed the boundary between worlds.

I turned and ran.

The sound of my footsteps echoed in the hallway as I fled, my breath coming in ragged gasps. Behind me, I could hear the faint, sickening sound of the figure moving, its body sliding through the mirror like some ancient, eldritch thing crawling out of the abyss. I didn't look back. I couldn't.

I reached my bedroom and slammed the door shut behind me, my hands shaking as I locked it. I stumbled back, pressing myself against the wall, my heart pounding in my chest as I listened. The house was silent again, but the silence was worse than any sound. It was the silence of a predator waiting in the dark, unseen, watching.

I don't know how long I stood there, pressed against the wall, my eyes fixed on the door, waiting for something to happen. But the door remained closed. The house remained quiet. There was no sign of the figure, no sound of movement, no whisper of the mirror.

And yet, I knew. I knew it was still there, somewhere in the house, waiting for me. The figure—the **doppelgänger**—had crossed over.

I had seen its face, its terrible, smiling face, and I knew it had seen mine. And now it was **loose** in my world.

Chapter 6: Escaping the Mirror World

The weight of the night before hung over me like a heavy shroud as I woke the next morning, though it was a shallow, fitful sleep that had claimed me. My body felt as though it had been dragged through an ocean of fear, leaving me drenched in dread that refused to evaporate with the rising sun. The events with the doppelgänger had left an imprint on my mind—no longer could I pretend that what I'd seen was just an illusion or a trick of the mind. The thing from the mirror was real, and worse still, it had crossed into my world.

I stood in my kitchen, a cup of cold coffee forgotten in my hand, my gaze fixed on the door to the study. I knew what awaited me beyond it, and the mere thought of confronting the mirror again filled me with a primal terror that gripped my chest and tightened with each passing second.

But I couldn't avoid it forever. The mirror had made that much clear.

Something had crossed over—something that did not belong in this world. Its presence lingered in the house, a palpable distortion in the air, a wrongness that I could feel deep within my bones. I couldn't see it, but I knew it was there, watching from the shadows, lurking just beyond the edge of perception.

I had to do something. I couldn't let it roam freely.

The thought of going back into the study made my stomach turn, but I had no choice. Whatever power the mirror held, I had to face it head-on. I had to understand it. Maybe, just maybe, I could find a way to stop it. Or at least, to stop the thing that had crawled out of it.

The house was eerily quiet as I approached the door to the study once more, my hand trembling on the doorknob. The same oppressive atmosphere awaited me on the other side—the same cold, suffocating sense of being watched. But this time, I couldn't shake the feeling that something far worse was waiting, something lurking behind the thin veil of reality.

I stepped inside, and my eyes immediately fell on the mirror. Its surface was dark, impossibly dark, as though it no longer reflected the room at all but instead absorbed it. There was no sign of my reflection, no indication of the doppelgänger, but the air was thick with its presence. I could feel it, like an open wound in the fabric of space.

I approached the mirror cautiously, every fiber of my being screaming at me to turn back, to run. But I couldn't. I was trapped, and I knew it. The mirror had me now. It was no longer just an object. It was a **door**—a door I had opened.

My breath caught in my throat as I stood before it, and once again, the surface began to ripple. The blackness deepened, and for a moment, I thought I saw something move behind the glass—a flicker, a shadow, just at the edge of perception.

Without thinking, I reached out and touched the surface.

My fingers sank into the glass.

It was like stepping into cold, viscous water, the sensation both chilling and unreal. The surface of the mirror gave way beneath my touch, and before I could react, I felt myself being pulled forward. My entire body plunged into the mirror, the world behind me dissolving into darkness, swallowed whole by the void.

I tumbled through that darkness for what felt like an eternity, my sense of self disintegrating as the oppressive weight of the mirror world pressed down on me. It was as though the very air had thickened into something solid, something alive. I could feel it pushing against me from all sides, pulling me deeper into its grasp, deeper into the **unknown**.

Then, just as suddenly as it had started, the sensation stopped.

I found myself standing in an alien landscape, though that word hardly did it justice. The world around me was a twisted mockery of reality—a place where the laws of nature held no sway, where the ground writhed like flesh and the sky churned with strange, unnatural colors. The horizon was distant, yet somehow close, warping in ways that made my head spin. It was as if I stood in a dimension where time and space themselves were fractured, bent to the will of some unseen force.

And all around me, I felt **it**—the presence that had crossed over from the mirror. But here, it was stronger. The very air seemed thick with its malice, its cold, malevolent awareness pressing down on me like a weight I could not escape.

The sky was alive, writhing with shapes I could barely comprehend—**things** that defied the natural order of the universe. Colossal figures moved just beyond the periphery of my vision, their forms constantly shifting, their outlines impossible to grasp. They were not of this world, nor of any world I had ever known. They were **ancient** and alien, their presence radiating an incomprehensible power that made my skin crawl.

I knew then that I had made a terrible mistake.

I had crossed into their world.

Panic surged through me as I realized the enormity of what I had done. This wasn't just another dimension—it was a place beyond the reach of human understanding, a realm where things older than time itself dwelled. And I had opened a door to it. Worse still, I had allowed something from this place to enter **my** world.

I had to get out. I had to escape.

I turned, frantically searching for the mirror, the only way back. But the landscape around me was constantly shifting, the ground beneath my feet twisting and warping as though it were alive. The mirror was gone, lost in the chaos of this maddening world. I was alone, trapped in a place where the very fabric of reality seemed to be unraveling.

As I stumbled forward, desperate to find some way out, the shadows around me began to move. They twisted and coiled, taking shape, becoming **figures**—tall, thin, and grotesque. Their bodies were composed of the same rippling blackness that filled the mirror, their limbs long and angular, their faces featureless. Yet I could feel their eyes on me, their unseen gaze burning into my skin.

They were the **watchers**, the things that lurked beyond the mirror, and now they were here, surrounding me, cutting off any chance of escape.

I backed away, my heart racing, but no matter where I turned, they were there—silent, watching, waiting. Their presence was suffocating, their forms distorting the very air around them, bending it to their will.

And then, from behind them, I saw it—the **doppelgänger**.

It stepped forward, emerging from the shadows like a predator stalking its prey. Its form was twisted, warped beyond recognition, yet I knew it was me—or at least, it was meant to be. Its face, once a perfect reflection of mine, had melted into something grotesque, its features elongated and stretched, its eyes filled with a cold, mocking hatred.

I stumbled back, but there was nowhere to go. The watchers pressed in closer, their forms shifting and twisting like smoke, blocking every path. I could feel the panic rising in my chest, my breath coming in short, ragged gasps as I realized the truth.

There was no escape.

I had crossed into the mirror world, and now the mirror world had me.

The doppelgänger stepped closer, its smile growing wider, more twisted, its eyes gleaming with malicious intent. It was the embodiment of everything that lurked in this dark, terrible place—a reflection not of me, but of the horrors that lived beyond the boundaries of reality.

I was **its** now.

Chapter 7: Nightmares and Paranoia

I didn't remember how I escaped the mirror world, or even if I had truly escaped at all. One moment I had been surrounded by the watchers and the doppelgänger, their oppressive presence crushing me, suffocating me. And then... I was back. Back in the house, back in my bed, drenched in sweat, my heart hammering in my chest as though it would tear itself free.

But something had changed.

The world around me felt thinner, as though the boundary between realities had stretched too far and now threatened to tear. The shadows in my room were too deep, too alive. Even the air felt wrong—heavier, colder. I stared at the ceiling, trying to convince myself that I was still in the waking world, but the more I looked, the less certain I became.

Had I truly returned? Or had I simply fallen deeper into the nightmare?

I sat up, my breath coming in shallow gasps, my pulse racing. The familiar contours of my room seemed to blur at the edges, twisting and shifting like the mirror world's alien landscape. The bed beneath me felt too soft, too yielding, as though the very structure of reality had begun to decay.

I stumbled out of bed, my legs trembling beneath me. I needed air, something to clear my head, something to remind me of the real world. I staggered to the window and threw it open, gasping as the cold night air rushed in.

Outside, the world seemed still. The trees stood motionless in the faint moonlight, their branches casting long shadows across the grass. But even as I watched, I could feel it—the sense of **wrongness** creeping at the edges of my perception. It was as though the very air outside had grown thick, distorted, as though the house itself had become a beacon for the horrors of the mirror world.

I leaned against the window frame, trying to calm my racing heart, but the more I tried to focus on the world outside, the more the shadows seemed to move, to shift. Shapes—vague, impossible shapes—seemed to flit through the trees, just out of sight. Too fast to catch, too dark to see clearly, but there.

My stomach lurched as I realized the truth.

The mirror world had followed me.

Whatever thin boundary had once separated the two worlds was now fragile, permeable. I could feel it in every breath, in every shadow. The things that had once been confined to the glass were now leaking into my reality, their presence like a stain spreading across the fabric of existence.

I stumbled back from the window, my legs weak, my mind racing with a thousand frantic thoughts. There was no escape. No matter how far I ran, no matter where I hid, the mirror world would find me. It had its claws in me now, and it would not let go.

I had opened the door, and now it was too late to close it.

I left the window open, the cold air a feeble comfort as I paced the room, trying to push away the growing sense of **paranoia**. My mind felt raw, exposed, every thought tinged with the creeping terror that something was watching me, following me, waiting for the moment to strike. I could feel it in the air around me, that oppressive weight that had been growing ever since I had first touched the mirror.

The **doppelgänger**.

It was still out there, somewhere in the house, lurking in the shadows, waiting for me to let my guard down. I had seen its face, its horrible twisted grin, and I knew it would not stop until it had taken my place. It wasn't just an imitation of me—it was something far worse, a being born of the mirror world, a **predator** that hunted in silence, unseen.

My head throbbed, my thoughts spiraling into an endless loop of fear and dread. I tried to convince myself that I was safe, that I was still in control. But deep down, I knew I wasn't. The mirror world had begun to infect my mind, twisting my perception of reality, turning every shadow into a potential threat.

I sat on the edge of the bed, burying my face in my hands. My pulse was racing, my thoughts spiraling out of control. I needed to think, needed to figure out how to stop this before it consumed me completely. But how could I fight something I couldn't even understand? How could I defend myself against a world that existed beyond the reach of human comprehension?

As I sat there, lost in the depths of my own fear, I heard it.

A sound.

Faint at first, barely a whisper, but growing louder with each passing second. It was coming from somewhere in the house, soft and insistent, like the slow creaking of old wood, or the shuffle of footsteps moving across the floor.

My blood turned to ice.

It was here. The doppelgänger.

I stood, my body trembling, my heart pounding in my chest. The sound grew louder, closer. I could hear it now—the distinct rhythm of footsteps, slow and deliberate, as though something was moving through the hallway just outside my room. My mind screamed at me to run, to flee, but my body refused to obey. I stood frozen, rooted to the spot, my breath caught in my throat.

The footsteps stopped.

For a long moment, there was only silence. The kind of silence that filled the air when a predator was about to pounce. I could feel it standing there, just beyond the door, waiting for me to make the first move.

I took a step back, my gaze locked on the door, half-expecting it to swing open at any moment. But it didn't. Instead, I heard a sound—a soft, almost **mocking** laugh.

It was my laugh.

My blood ran cold. It was the doppelgänger. It had learned my voice, my laughter, and now it was using them against me.

The door remained closed, but I could feel its presence on the other side, waiting for me to let my guard down, to open the door and let it in. It was toying with me, playing some twisted game. But I wasn't ready to lose. Not yet.

I couldn't stay in the room. I had to move, had to do something. Anything. I couldn't let it trap me like this.

With trembling hands, I reached for the window and climbed through it, dropping to the ground outside. The cold night air stung my skin, but the sensation was a welcome reminder that I was still in the real world, still tethered to reality—however fragile that tether had become.

I glanced back at the house, my eyes searching the dark windows for any sign of movement. But there was nothing. No shadows, no flickers of light. Just the oppressive stillness that had become all too familiar.

I walked quickly, my steps uneven, my pulse racing as I moved away from the house, away from the thing that now hunted me. I didn't know where I was going, didn't care. All I knew was that I had to get away from the mirror, from the doppelgänger, from whatever was waiting for me in the depths of the house.

The night was thick with shadows, the trees looming overhead like skeletal sentinels. Every rustle of leaves, every faint breeze, sent a jolt of fear through me. My mind was playing tricks on me now, turning every sound, every movement, into a potential threat. I could feel my sanity slipping, the line between reality and the mirror world growing thinner with every step I took.

The paranoia had taken root, and there was no escape.

Chapter 8: First Reflection

The night stretched on, endless and oppressive. I wandered the streets, the cold biting at my skin, but it wasn't enough to pierce the fog that had settled over my mind. The world felt distant, unfamiliar, as though I had stepped into a dream from which I couldn't wake. Every streetlight cast long, twisted shadows that flickered and danced at the edges of my vision. The sounds of the night—rustling leaves, distant cars—were muffled, as if I were hearing them from underwater.

I had fled the house, but I knew it wouldn't be enough. The doppelgänger was still there, waiting, watching. I had escaped its immediate grasp, but how long could I run? How long could I stay ahead of it? The paranoia gnawed at me, every shadow feeling like it hid the thing that had crawled out of the mirror.

I found myself standing in front of a run-down diner, its flickering neon sign buzzing in the stillness of the night. I didn't know why I had come here—perhaps it was some primal instinct, a need to be around other people, to convince myself that the world still existed beyond the boundaries of the house and the mirror. I pushed open the door and stepped inside, the warm light and faint hum of conversation briefly disorienting me after the cold emptiness of the streets.

The diner was nearly empty, just a few patrons scattered at the counter, heads down over their coffee or meals. I slid into a booth at the far end, my back pressed against the worn leather seat, my eyes flicking to every reflective surface in the room. The windows, the stainless-steel coffee machine, even the polished chrome napkin holders—they all gleamed with faint reflections, distorted and warped by the light.

I couldn't escape it. The mirror world had infected everything.

A waitress approached, her eyes tired but kind as she held a notepad in her hand. "What can I get you, hon?" she asked, her voice a faint comfort in the overwhelming terror that gnawed at my insides.

"Just... just coffee," I managed to say, my voice shaky. I barely met her gaze, my eyes constantly darting to the reflections around me.

She nodded and shuffled away, and I leaned forward, my hands shaking as they rested on the table. The cold paranoia gripped me tighter, the sense that I wasn't alone here, that **it** was still watching me, still hunting me. I glanced at the reflective surfaces again, half-expecting to see my own face staring back at me, twisted into that same malicious grin I had seen in the mirror.

But something else caught my attention instead.

The man sitting at the counter, just a few seats away from the waitress, was staring into the reflection of the chrome napkin holder in front of him. At first, I thought nothing of it. But then he turned slightly, just enough for me to see his face.

My heart stopped.

It was **me**.

Not someone who looked like me. Not a stranger with similar features. It was **exactly** me. The same eyes, the same hair, the same clothes I had been wearing earlier in the night. The man at the counter was my perfect double, sitting there as if he had always been there, staring blankly at his reflection.

I froze, unable to breathe, my heart pounding in my chest as the reality of what I was seeing settled over me like a suffocating weight. The doppelgänger had found me. It had followed me here.

The man—**the thing**—slowly turned his head, his eyes meeting mine across the diner. For a long, agonizing moment, we stared at each other, and I could feel the same malevolent energy radiating from him that I had felt in the mirror. His expression was calm, almost neutral, but there was something lurking just beneath the surface, something cold and calculating, something that made my skin crawl.

I stood abruptly, knocking over my coffee cup in the process. The waitress looked over, startled, but I couldn't focus on her. My eyes were locked on the doppelgänger as it rose from the counter, mirroring my movements exactly. It was like looking into a twisted funhouse mirror—every motion it made was too perfect, too exact, and yet I knew it wasn't **me**. It was an imitation, a predator wearing my face.

I backed away toward the door, my breath coming in shallow gasps. The other patrons hadn't noticed the doppelgänger, hadn't seen the terror unfolding just feet away from them. They were oblivious, lost in their own lives, unaware of the cosmic horror that had slipped into their world.

The doppelgänger took a step forward, and for the first time, it **smiled**—that same horrible, twisted grin that I had seen in the mirror, the same smile that had haunted my every step since the moment I touched the glass. It wasn't just a smile of mockery. It was a promise. A promise that no matter where I ran, no matter how far I tried to escape, it would always find me.

I turned and bolted for the door, the cool night air slapping me in the face as I stumbled out into the street. My legs felt weak, my vision blurred by panic as I ran down the empty sidewalks, my footsteps echoing in the quiet. But no matter how fast I ran, I could feel it behind me, following me, its presence pressing against my back like a shadow I couldn't shake.

The buildings loomed around me, their dark windows like the eyes of the mirror world, watching my every move. My heart pounded in my chest, my lungs burning with each ragged breath, but I couldn't stop. I had to get away. I had to **hide**.

But where? Where could I go where the doppelgänger wouldn't follow? Every corner I turned, every alley I ducked into, I felt its presence closing in, like the walls of the world itself were tightening around me, leaving me no room to escape.

I stumbled into a narrow alleyway and collapsed against the cold brick wall, my breath coming in short, panicked gasps. My vision swam, and for a moment, I thought I could see the reflection of the doppelgänger in the glass of a nearby window, its face grinning at me from the shadows.

I shut my eyes tightly, willing the image away. But when I opened them again, it was still there. The doppelgänger, standing at the mouth of the alley, staring at me with those cold, empty eyes, its smile growing wider and wider as it slowly stepped toward me.

I tried to scream, but no sound came out. I tried to run, but my legs refused to move. I was paralyzed by fear, frozen in place as the doppelgänger advanced, its twisted form seeming to blur and warp with every step it took.

And then, as it stood just inches from me, it whispered in a voice that was my own: "You can't run from me."

It reached out, its fingers long and thin, and for a moment, I thought I could feel the cold touch of its hand on my skin.

Then everything went black.

Chapter 9: The First Trap

When I awoke, the world around me was shrouded in a thick, oppressive fog. My head throbbed with a dull, insistent pain, and it took a moment for me to gather my bearings, to remember where I was—or even who I was. The events of the previous night returned in disjointed flashes: the diner, the doppelgänger, its cold, mocking smile, and the alleyway where everything had gone black.

I slowly sat up, my body aching from the frantic chase. The alley was still around me, its narrow walls pressing in like the jaws of some monstrous creature. The dim light of dawn filtered through the fog, casting long, eerie shadows that seemed to stretch and warp as if they had a life of their own. I shivered, the cold seeping into my bones, but the chill that gripped me went deeper than the temperature. It was the same dread I had felt since the mirror had first called to me—the same sense that I was being watched by something far beyond my understanding.

I stood, my legs unsteady beneath me, and glanced around the alley. For a brief, desperate moment, I thought maybe the doppelgänger had finally left me, that I was free. But as I looked into the mist, I saw it.

A shadow. A figure, standing at the end of the alley, still and silent, watching.

It was **me**.

The doppelgänger, unmoving, its eyes locked onto mine. Even in the dim light, I could see the glint of its twisted smile, the way it tilted its head ever so slightly, as if to mock my fear.

I backed away, my heart racing, my breath coming in shallow gasps. My mind screamed at me to run, but where could I go? How could I escape something that could follow me anywhere? Something that had my face, my voice, my very being?

Then, as if reading my thoughts, the doppelgänger stepped forward, slowly, deliberately, its footsteps soundless in the fog. It moved with an unnatural grace, its body shifting slightly with each step, as though the very fabric of reality bent around it.

I turned and fled, my feet pounding against the pavement, the cold air burning my lungs as I pushed myself to move faster. The streets were deserted, the city still wrapped in the early morning quiet, but I could feel the doppelgänger behind me, always there, always following. No matter how fast I ran, no matter how many corners I turned, it was there.

The streets twisted and turned, unfamiliar now. I had no sense of direction, no idea where I was headed—only that I had to keep moving. The fog thickened, swallowing up the buildings and lampposts, turning the city into a maze of shadows and indistinct shapes. Every sound was muffled, distant, as though I had crossed into another world entirely.

Then, out of the fog, I saw it.

A doorway.

It was an old, heavy wooden door set into the side of a crumbling building, half-hidden by the mist. I didn't think—didn't stop to question why it was there, or why it felt so out of place. All I knew was that I had to get away from the doppelgänger, and this door was the only chance I had.

I reached for the handle and yanked the door open, slipping inside just as the doppelgänger emerged from the fog behind me. I slammed the door shut, my breath coming in ragged gasps as I pressed my back against the rough wood, praying that it wouldn't follow me through.

For a moment, there was silence.

Then I heard it—the soft, deliberate sound of footsteps on the other side of the door. I pressed myself harder against the wood, willing it to hold, to keep the thing out. The footsteps grew louder, closer, and then stopped just on the other side.

I held my breath, my heart hammering in my chest.

The door remained closed. The footsteps did not continue.

I exhaled slowly, cautiously, and turned to face the room I had entered. It was a small, dimly lit space, filled with the faint scent of dust and mildew. A single, flickering lightbulb hung from the ceiling, casting long shadows that seemed to writhe and twist with the movement of the light.

But what caught my attention immediately was the **mirror**.

It stood in the center of the room, tall and imposing, its dark surface reflecting the dim light of the bulb. The sight of it made my stomach drop, and a cold dread settled over me. I had seen enough mirrors to know that this was not a coincidence.

This was a **trap**.

I should have turned and run. I should have thrown the door open and fled back into the fog, back into the streets. But I didn't. The mirror had me now. It had drawn me in, and I could feel its pull, the same pull that had gripped me the first time I had touched the mirror in my study.

The air in the room was thick with the same oppressive weight I had felt in the mirror world. I could feel it pressing down on me, making it hard to breathe, hard to think. My legs felt heavy, my body sluggish, as though the very air was trying to hold me in place, to keep me here.

And then I saw it.

My **reflection**.

It stood there in the glass, watching me, its eyes dark and empty, its face blank and emotionless. At first, it was just a reflection, just an image of myself standing in the room. But then, slowly, its expression began to change.

A smile crept across its face—slow, deliberate, that same horrible, twisted smile that the doppelgänger had worn. My heart raced, my breath catching in my throat as I stared at it, unable to tear my eyes away.

The reflection took a step forward, moving closer to the surface of the mirror, its eyes locked on mine. It raised its hand, pressing it against the glass, just as the doppelgänger had done. And as it moved, I could see something else in the reflection—something **behind me**.

I turned, my heart pounding, but the room was empty. There was nothing there. No one.

But when I looked back at the mirror, I saw it again.

The reflection of something in the shadows. Something twisted and grotesque, its limbs long and angular, its face a mass of shifting darkness. It was watching me from the corners of the room, hidden in the gloom, but I could feel its gaze, cold and malevolent, boring into me.

I stumbled back, my pulse racing, and the reflection in the mirror grinned wider, its eyes gleaming with dark amusement. The thing behind me—the thing in the shadows—moved closer, its shape flickering at the edge of my vision.

Panic surged through me. I had to get out. I had to get away.

I turned toward the door, but it was gone.

The room had changed. The door that I had entered through was no longer there—just a blank, empty wall where it had once been. I was trapped, caught in the web that the mirror had spun.

I spun back toward the mirror, and the reflection of the thing in the shadows was closer now. I could see it more clearly, its body hunched and twisted, its eyes glowing faintly in the darkness. It reached out with long, skeletal fingers, as though to pull me into the glass.

My reflection stepped back, and the smile faded from its face. It stared at me with cold, empty eyes, waiting, watching.

I had fallen into the trap. The mirror world had me now, and there was no escape.

Chapter 10: The First Trap Tightens

Panic clawed at my chest like some monstrous thing trying to break free as I stood before the mirror, trapped in that room without a door. The thing in the reflection loomed closer, its grotesque, twisted form shifting in the darkness like smoke. Its limbs were impossibly long, its face a writhing mass of shadow and sharp angles that defied any logic or sense of reality. I couldn't see its eyes, but I could **feel** them—feel the weight of its gaze pressing down on me, hungry and cold, as if it was sizing me up for the inevitable.

I tried to move, but my body felt heavy, sluggish. My legs wobbled beneath me, and my breath came in ragged, shallow gasps. The air in the room was thick, oppressive, as though I had been buried alive. The mirror's pull was stronger than ever now, a gravitational force that seemed to bend the very space around me.

My reflection, still standing in the glass, watched me with a blank, unblinking stare. The smile that had once curled across its lips had vanished, replaced by something far worse: **indifference**. It no longer mirrored my movements or emotions; it was a separate entity now, observing me like a predator watching its prey, waiting for the right moment to strike.

I backed away from the mirror, my pulse racing, but the thing in the reflection—the **thing** lurking in the shadows—moved closer. Its body twisted and contorted, slipping through the darkness with an unnatural grace that made my skin crawl. It was as though the laws of nature didn't apply to it, as though it existed outside of the reality I knew. The way it moved, the way it **stretched** and **shifted**, was wrong in ways I couldn't fully comprehend.

I turned in place, searching for a way out, but the walls of the room had closed in around me. There was no escape, no exit, no door. The very fabric of the room seemed to warp and twist, as though the mirror was slowly consuming it, turning everything into its own reflection, into its own distorted version of reality. The walls, the floor, the very air felt **thinner**, less real, as though the mirror was sucking the life out of the space.

I stumbled backward, my back pressing against the cold wall, and my mind raced through a thousand frantic thoughts. The mirror wanted me. The thing in the reflection wanted me. It had been hunting me since the moment I first touched the mirror in my home, and now, now it had me trapped. Now, it would take me.

I felt a sudden jolt of clarity.

I couldn't let it.

I had come too far, fought too hard. I wasn't going to let this thing—this **reflection**, this twisted version of myself—consume me. I wasn't going to let it win. The mirror had brought me into its world, into its trap, but it wasn't invincible. If it could pull me in, maybe I could find a way to push back. Maybe, just maybe, I could fight it.

The thing in the reflection was closer now, its body sliding through the glass like oil through water. I could see its form more clearly—the sharp, angular limbs, the shifting, writhing shadows that made up its face. Its presence filled the room like a physical weight, and I could feel its cold breath on my skin, hear the faint whisper of its movements.

I looked down at my hands, trembling with fear and adrenaline. I had no weapon, no way to fight this thing physically, but maybe... maybe I didn't need one. This wasn't just a physical battle—it was a battle of the mind, of will. The mirror had been manipulating me from the start, pulling me deeper into its world, using my own fear against me. But what if I could turn that against it?

I stepped forward, closer to the mirror, and my reflection tilted its head ever so slightly, as if curious about my actions. The thing in the shadows stopped moving, waiting, watching.

I took another step, and another, until I was standing just inches from the surface of the mirror. I could see my reflection staring back at me, the blank, emotionless face that was no longer mine. The thing behind it was still there, lurking in the dark, its form flickering like a dying flame.

I raised my hand, fingers trembling, and pressed it against the glass.

The surface of the mirror rippled beneath my touch, just as it had before, but this time, something was different. The mirror **pushed back**.

I could feel it, feel the cold, malevolent force pressing against my hand, trying to pull me in. But I pushed harder. I focused all of my energy, all of my fear, into that single point of contact. I could feel the mirror straining, feel the glass bending under the weight of my will.

And then, just for a moment, the glass **cracked**.

It was faint, almost imperceptible, but I heard it—the sound of the mirror **breaking** under the pressure. A hairline fracture appeared, spreading across the surface like a spider's web. The thing in the reflection twitched, its body jerking as if in pain, its expression flickering between indifference and something else—something like fear.

I pressed harder, my hand digging into the glass, and the crack spread further. The thing in the shadows recoiled, pulling back into the darkness, its form distorting and warping as though the mirror's power was being drained.

For the first time since this nightmare began, I felt a glimmer of hope.

The mirror could be **broken**.

The reflection hissed, a low, guttural sound that vibrated through the glass, and for a brief moment, I saw something shift in its eyes—something **inhuman**, something that wasn't just a part of the mirror, but something older, something that had existed long before I had ever touched the glass. I realized then that the reflection wasn't just a doppelgänger. It was a part of the mirror world itself, a manifestation of the ancient, malevolent force that had created the mirror. It was a fragment of something far greater, something far worse.

And now, it was weakening.

The mirror cracked again, the fracture spreading like a jagged scar across the surface. The air in the room grew colder, heavier, as though the very space around me was **tearing** apart, unraveling. I could feel the pull of the mirror growing stronger, but it wasn't pulling me in anymore. It was pulling **itself** apart.

The thing in the shadows let out a high-pitched screech, a sound that reverberated through my skull, and I stumbled back, my hand slipping from the glass. The reflection staggered, its form flickering like a dying flame, its smile twisted into something far more grotesque and desperate.

I had weakened it, but it wasn't over. Not yet.

The mirror was still **alive**, still fighting to pull me back in, to trap me within its twisted reality. The cracks in the glass spread further, but they hadn't shattered it completely. I had to finish this. I had to break the mirror, once and for all.

I looked around the room, frantic, searching for something—anything—that I could use to destroy the mirror. My eyes landed on a heavy, rusted iron candlestick resting on a nearby table. Without thinking, I grabbed it, my hands shaking with adrenaline, and raised it above my head.

The reflection's eyes widened in horror, its face twisting into a mask of pure rage and desperation. The thing in the shadows screeched again, its form writhing and contorting as it tried to pull itself back through the glass.

With a final, desperate cry, I brought the candlestick down onto the mirror.

The glass shattered.

A deafening crack echoed through the room as the mirror splintered into a thousand jagged shards, the fragments raining down around me like pieces of broken reality. The force of the impact sent me stumbling back, my breath coming in ragged gasps as I watched the mirror **collapse** in on itself, its surface folding inward, warping and twisting like a vortex.

The reflection let out one final, agonized scream, and then it was **gone**. The room around me shook violently, the walls and floor warping and shifting as the mirror world collapsed, pulling itself back into the void.

I fell to my knees, exhausted, my body trembling from the effort. The room was quiet now, eerily still. The oppressive weight that had filled the air was gone, replaced by an almost serene calm.

The mirror was broken.

But I knew, deep down, that this wasn't the end. The mirror world wasn't destroyed. It had merely **retreated**—for now.

And somewhere, out there in the shadows, the doppelgänger was still waiting.

Chapter 11: Time and Memory Distortion

After the mirror shattered and the thing from the reflection disappeared, I expected relief. I expected the crushing dread that had settled over me for so long to finally lift. But the eerie calm that followed the destruction of the mirror was not the peace I had hoped for. It was something worse—an unnatural silence, as if the world itself was **holding its breath**, waiting for something even more terrible to unfold.

I stood in the ruined room, my body trembling with exhaustion and fear. The shattered pieces of the mirror lay scattered at my feet, each shard reflecting a fragmented version of the room—disjointed images that made my stomach churn. As I looked down at the broken glass, a sinking realization crept over me: though the mirror was destroyed, its influence had not ended.

In the fragments of glass, I saw **my reflection** staring back at me, but it wasn't quite right. The images in the shards flickered and shifted as though each piece reflected a different version of me—a different moment in time. In one shard, I looked younger, almost childlike, my face pale and frightened. In another, I was older, my skin lined with age and weariness. These fractured reflections weren't just reflections of me now; they were **versions of me that didn't exist** in this moment.

It felt as if time itself had fractured along with the mirror, splintering into countless threads that now surrounded me, pulling me in different directions. The air around me felt thick, as though I were walking through water, and my thoughts became foggy, jumbled. The room shifted and warped, the walls stretching out one moment, closing in the next, as though space and time no longer followed any rules I could understand.

I stumbled forward, nearly tripping over the pieces of the mirror as I moved toward the wall where the door should have been. But the door was still gone. The room had no exits now, no way out. I was **trapped** in this collapsing space, a prisoner of time itself.

I glanced down at my hands. They were trembling, but worse still, they were **changing**. One moment they looked as they always had—calloused from years of living. The next, they were soft, unmarked, like a child's hands. Then, they were wrinkled, aged beyond recognition. I watched in horror as my body shifted and morphed, as if I were being pulled through different moments in my own life, torn between past and future.

The dizziness grew stronger, and I collapsed to my knees, clutching my head as memories began to flood my mind—memories that weren't my own, or at least, not memories that should have been mine. I saw flashes of moments from my childhood, events I had long forgotten, twisted and distorted by the mirror's influence. I saw myself as a child, standing in front of a mirror that shouldn't have existed in my home, its dark surface watching me even then.

Then, there were memories from the **future**, moments that hadn't happened yet but felt terrifyingly real. I saw myself growing older, alone, living in a house filled with mirrors, each one reflecting the horrors of the mirror world. I saw myself consumed by the very thing I had tried to destroy, my body twisted and broken, a prisoner of the reflection that had once been mine.

These memories weren't just **visions**. They felt real, as if I were living them, as if I were being torn from one moment to the next without any control over my own life.

I tried to focus, to pull myself back into the present, but the present had become slippery, elusive. My mind was trapped between these fractured moments, these shards of time that had shattered along with the mirror. Every time I tried to anchor myself in reality, I was pulled into another memory, another version of myself, each more distorted than the last.

I screamed, clutching my head as the flood of memories overwhelmed me. Faces I recognized—my family, my friends—swirled through my mind, their features warping and changing as if the mirror world was rewriting my history, rewriting **me**.

And then, through the chaos, I heard a voice.

It was faint at first, barely a whisper, but it cut through the noise in my mind like a knife. I recognized the voice immediately—it was **mine**. Not the voice I spoke with now, but the voice from the **reflection**. The doppelgänger.

"You can't hide from me."

The words echoed in my mind, cold and mocking, as if the doppelgänger was still there, still watching me from the broken pieces of the mirror. I glanced down again at the shards scattered across the floor, and in each one, I saw **its face** staring back at me, grinning that horrible, twisted grin. It hadn't gone away. The mirror was broken, but the reflection remained. It was still here, still part of me, still **inside** me.

Panic surged through me as I realized the truth. Breaking the mirror hadn't freed me—it had only made things worse. Now, the doppelgänger wasn't confined to the glass. It had spread, fracturing along with time itself, embedding itself in every moment, every version of me. It was no longer a separate entity. It was me, living in every possible reality, every possible version of my life.

I stumbled to my feet, desperate to escape the room, to escape the mirror's influence, but there was nowhere to go. The walls seemed to close in on me, shifting and warping with each passing second. Time and space had become fluid, folding in on themselves, trapping me in this endless loop of fragmented memories.

I had to find a way out. I had to break free before the doppelgänger consumed me completely, before I lost myself in the tangled web of time. But how? The mirror was gone, and yet its power lingered, wrapping itself around me like a noose tightening with every breath I took.

I reached out, my hand brushing against the wall, and for a moment, I felt something—**a door**. It was faint, barely there, as though it existed in another moment, another version of the room. But I could feel it, and I knew that if I could just focus, if I could just **find** the present, I might be able to escape.

I closed my eyes, trying to block out the flood of memories, trying to ground myself in the here and now. The doppelgänger's voice echoed in my mind, taunting me, trying to pull me back into the endless cycle of fractured time. But I fought against it, clinging to the faint sensation of the door, willing it to be real.

THE SPACE BETWEEN THE MIRROR

Slowly, the memories began to fade, the disjointed flashes of past and future receding into the background. I focused on my breathing, on the feel of the cold wall beneath my fingers, and little by little, the present began to solidify around me.

The room stopped shifting. The air grew still.

I opened my eyes.

The door was there.

It was real.

Without hesitating, I grabbed the handle and pulled it open, stumbling through into the hallway beyond. The moment I crossed the threshold, the oppressive weight of the mirror world lifted, and I gasped, feeling the cool air of reality wash over me.

I was out.

I collapsed against the wall, my body trembling with exhaustion, my mind still reeling from the flood of distorted memories. But I was out. I was free.

Or so I thought.

As I stood there, trying to catch my breath, I glanced back at the room I had just escaped. The shattered pieces of the mirror lay scattered across the floor, reflecting the dim light from the hallway.

And in one of the shards, I saw it.

The doppelgänger.

Its face, still twisted into that horrible grin, watching me from the glass.

Waiting.

Chapter 12: Encountering the Eyeless Figures

I stumbled down the hallway, my legs barely able to carry me. The oppressive weight of the mirror's presence still clung to me, though its physical form was gone. My mind spun, fragmented by the disjointed flashes of time and memory that I had just experienced. The hallway stretched before me, seemingly endless, its dim lights flickering like dying embers. Each step I took echoed in the silence, reverberating like a slow drumbeat in the stillness of the house.

Had I really escaped?

Even as the thought crossed my mind, a cold dread sank into my gut. I could still feel it—that **watching**, that same terrible presence I had felt in the mirror world. Though I was no longer trapped in that twisted room, the world around me felt wrong, as if the mirror's influence had seeped into everything. The walls seemed to breathe, the air too thick, too heavy.

And then I felt it—**them**.

The air around me shifted, cold and unnatural, as though something had slipped into the space beside me. I froze, my breath catching in my throat, every instinct in my body screaming to **run**, to get away. But I couldn't move. My feet felt rooted to the floor, as if the very ground beneath me had turned to quicksand, pulling me down into its suffocating embrace.

Slowly, I turned my head, my pulse pounding in my ears.

At first, I saw nothing. Just the dimly lit hallway stretching out into darkness. But then, from the shadows, they emerged. The **Eyeless Figures**.

There were three of them, standing at the far end of the hallway, their bodies tall and unnaturally thin. Their skin was pale, almost translucent, and their faces... their faces were **smooth**, featureless, devoid of any eyes, nose, or mouth. Just blank, empty surfaces where their features should have been. They stood completely still, their heads slightly tilted as if listening for something, even though they had no ears. Their presence filled the air with an unbearable sense of **wrongness**, a perversion of what should exist.

I tried to back away, my heart hammering in my chest, but the moment I moved, their heads snapped toward me in unison.

My breath hitched in my throat, and I froze, staring at them, waiting for them to move, to do **something**. But they didn't. They simply stood there, their faceless heads turned in my direction, as though they could somehow **see** me despite having no eyes. Their presence was overwhelming, like a void that swallowed up all the light and sound in the room.

For a moment, we stood there, locked in a silent standoff, and I felt the hairs on the back of my neck rise. The Eyeless Figures did nothing, said nothing. They didn't need to. Their very existence was an affront to the natural order, a cold reminder that the world I had once known no longer obeyed the rules I understood.

And then, slowly, they began to move.

Their movements were jerky, unnatural, as though they were marionettes controlled by an unseen puppeteer. Their limbs bent at odd angles as they stepped forward, closing the distance between us with deliberate slowness, their heads still tilted in that unnatural way. Though they made no sound, I could feel their presence growing stronger, their void-like existence pressing against the edges of my mind, threatening to overwhelm me.

Panic surged through me, and I backed away, my legs trembling beneath me. The hallway seemed to **shift** around me, elongating as I moved, making it feel as though I were running in place. The Eyeless Figures continued their slow, methodical approach, their faceless heads never turning away from me.

I had to get away. I had to escape.

But there was nowhere to go.

As I backed further down the hallway, I heard a faint sound—a soft whisper, barely audible, like the rustle of wind through dead leaves. At first, I thought it was coming from the figures, but then I realized it was coming from **within me**.

It was the **doppelgänger**.

"You'll never escape," it whispered, the voice cold and mocking, the same voice I had heard when I'd shattered the mirror. "They've always been watching. They always will."

I clutched my head, trying to push the voice away, but it only grew louder, more insistent. The whisper wound through my thoughts like a poisonous thread, weaving itself into every corner of my mind. The Eyeless Figures continued to advance, their movements slow but relentless, their presence crushing the air from my lungs.

I turned and ran.

I didn't care that the hallway stretched impossibly before me, that the space itself seemed to warp and bend. I didn't care that the Eyeless Figures were always just behind me, moving with that same eerie slowness. All I knew was that I had to get away, had to find some escape, some way out of this nightmare.

But no matter how far I ran, I could feel them.

They were always just behind me, their faceless heads tilted in my direction, their silent steps echoing in the empty space. I could feel the cold void of their presence growing stronger, filling the air with an unbearable weight. And with each step I took, the whisper of the doppelgänger grew louder, more insistent.

"You can't outrun them," it hissed. "They see you, even without eyes. They know you. They've been waiting for you."

I stumbled, my breath ragged, my chest burning with every frantic gasp. I could feel the weight of the Eyeless Figures bearing down on me, could feel the icy grip of their presence wrapping around my mind, suffocating me. The hallway stretched on, endless and distorted, and I knew I couldn't keep running. I couldn't escape them.

And then, out of the corner of my eye, I saw something—a **door**. It was faint, barely visible in the distorted space of the hallway, but it was there, just ahead. A chance for escape.

I lunged toward it, my heart pounding in my chest, and grabbed the handle. The door swung open, and I threw myself through it, stumbling into the room beyond.

I slammed the door shut behind me, my breath coming in ragged gasps as I leaned against it, my body trembling with exhaustion. For a long moment, there was nothing but silence. The oppressive weight of the Eyeless Figures had vanished, replaced by a heavy stillness that settled over the room like a suffocating blanket.

I was alone.

Or at least, I thought I was.

I straightened, my breath still shaky, and looked around the room. It was small and dimly lit, the air thick with dust and neglect. There was a single window on the far wall, its glass cracked and dirty, letting in only the faintest sliver of light. The rest of the room was bare, empty except for a large, old mirror that stood in the corner.

My stomach twisted.

Another **mirror**.

I backed away from it, my pulse racing as the memories of the mirror world flooded back. I wanted to run, to flee from the room, but I knew it was too late. The mirror had found me again.

And then, as I stood there, frozen with fear, I saw it.

In the reflection of the mirror, I saw the **Eyeless Figures**.

They were behind me, their blank faces turned toward me, their bodies standing still and silent in the room. They hadn't followed me through the door, but somehow, they had found their way into the reflection.

I turned around, but the room was empty.

The Eyeless Figures weren't there. Only their reflections.

But they were watching.

Always watching.

Chapter 13: Psychological Breakdown

I could feel myself unraveling.

The Eyeless Figures had vanished from the room's physical space, but their presence lingered in the reflection, always hovering at the edges of my mind. As I stared at the cracked, dusty mirror in the corner of the room, my body shivered with an inexplicable cold. The thin slice of light from the broken window barely illuminated anything beyond a weak, sickly glow, and the shadows in the room seemed to swell with every passing moment. I couldn't tell whether they were growing or if my vision was simply distorting—yet another symptom of my deteriorating sanity.

I backed away from the mirror slowly, my pulse racing, each step feeling heavier than the last. My breath came in shallow, uneven gasps, and the walls seemed to close in, tightening the space until it felt as though I was being squeezed by the room itself. There was no escape—not from this room, not from the mirrors, and certainly not from the terrible, encroaching **presence** that had seeped into every corner of my reality.

I slumped against the wall, my body trembling with fear and exhaustion. My mind was breaking—splitting apart under the weight of everything I'd experienced. The memories, the distorted reflections of my life, the whispers of the doppelgänger, and the haunting gaze of the Eyeless Figures all swirled in a chaotic whirlwind inside my head.

Was any of it even real?

I closed my eyes, trying to focus, to ground myself. But even in the darkness behind my eyelids, the mirror world lurked, its twisted shapes and impossible geometry waiting to pull me back in. Flashes of that alien landscape, with its churning sky and grotesque creatures, flickered in and out of my mind, refusing to let go. I couldn't tell if I was still in the real world or if I'd fallen into the mirror again, trapped in some endless loop of horror.

I opened my eyes.

The mirror was still there, but now the reflection had shifted. The room looked the same, but I wasn't in the reflection anymore. Instead, the **Eyeless Figures** stood in my place, their faceless heads turned toward me, watching, always watching. They seemed to fill the room, their bodies motionless but their presence suffocating. And even though they had no eyes, I could feel them seeing into me, penetrating my mind, peering into the deepest, darkest parts of my soul.

I couldn't look at them anymore. I turned my gaze away from the mirror, my heart pounding in my chest, and I curled into myself, trying to block out the mounting panic. But the whispers wouldn't stop. The **doppelgänger's voice** was still there, coiling through my thoughts like a snake, slithering into every corner of my mind.

"You're unraveling," it whispered. "You've lost control. You never had it to begin with."

I pressed my hands to my head, trying to drown out the voice, trying to hold on to the last threads of my sanity. But it was slipping away, fragmenting like the mirror had shattered. I was breaking down, piece by piece, my identity splintering into a million reflections.

"You think you can escape this?" The doppelgänger's voice was louder now, more insistent, as if it were speaking directly into my ear. "There's no escape. There's never been an escape. You opened the door, and now you'll never close it. You're part of this now. You're **mine**."

I squeezed my eyes shut, my breath coming in shallow gasps, but the voice persisted, growing louder, more invasive. I could feel it digging into my mind, warping my sense of reality, bending the world around me. My memories, my identity—everything was being twisted, reshaped by the doppelgänger's influence.

"I'm you," it hissed. "Don't you see? You let me in. You let me become you."

I shook my head, trying to deny it, trying to fight it off. But it was no use. The lines between myself and the doppelgänger were blurring. I couldn't tell where I ended and where **it** began. The cold, hollow emptiness I had felt when I first saw it in the mirror had now taken root in me. It was inside me—growing, consuming me from the inside out.

The room seemed to pulse with the beat of my racing heart. The shadows swirled and flickered, warping into grotesque shapes that twisted and writhed at the edges of my vision. The walls seemed to undulate, as if the very space I occupied was **alive**, breathing, shifting with the will of the mirror world.

I glanced back at the mirror, unable to resist the pull of its dark surface. The Eyeless Figures were still there, but now they had begun to move—slowly, deliberately. Their limbs jerked and twisted as they took faltering steps toward the glass, their faceless heads still tilted toward me, as if they were trying to find me, to cross the boundary between their world and mine.

And behind them, I saw it.

The **doppelgänger**.

It stood in the shadows, half-hidden behind the Eyeless Figures, but I could see it clearly now. It was no longer an imitation of me—it had become something far worse. Its body was distorted, stretched and twisted into a grotesque parody of my own form. Its eyes were dark, empty voids, and its mouth was twisted into a mockery of a smile, jagged and too wide.

It stepped forward, pushing past the Eyeless Figures as it approached the mirror's surface. I watched, helpless, as it raised a hand to the glass, pressing its fingers against the reflection. The surface of the mirror rippled beneath its touch, and I could feel the pressure of its presence building in the room, suffocating me.

"You're losing yourself," it whispered, its voice echoing in my mind. "Piece by piece, you're becoming me."

I backed away from the mirror, my heart racing, my mind screaming in panic. I had to get out of here. I had to escape, had to find some way to stop this before it was too late. But there was no escape. The room had no doors, no windows. The mirror was the only way out, and it was already pulling me back in, drawing me deeper into its twisted world.

I could feel the doppelgänger's presence growing stronger, its influence spreading through my mind like a virus, infecting my thoughts, my memories. I wasn't sure who I was anymore. Was I still me, or was I becoming **it**?

Desperate, I lunged toward the mirror, my hand reaching for the surface. The glass rippled beneath my touch, just as it had before, and for a moment, I thought I could feel something—something familiar. My own reflection, buried beneath the layers of distortion, trying to break free.

But it was too late.

The doppelgänger's twisted form pressed against the glass, and I felt the mirror pull me in, dragging me back into the darkness.

The world around me shattered.

Chapter 14: Through the Shattered Glass

The world around me shattered like fragile glass.

One moment, I was standing in that suffocating room, pressed against the wall, staring at the doppelgänger as it slowly pressed its way through the mirror. The next, the ground seemed to fall away beneath me, and I was **falling**, tumbling through an endless void of broken reflections and twisted memories. It was as though the mirror had shattered reality itself, dragging me into its fragmented, distorted realm.

I couldn't breathe. I couldn't see. The darkness was everywhere, wrapping around me like a shroud. But within that darkness, I saw flashes—brief, agonizing moments of light that revealed pieces of something far worse. The Eyeless Figures were there, their forms drifting through the void like pale phantoms, their faceless heads turning slowly as they passed me by, as if they were searching for something—or someone.

And always, there was the **doppelgänger**.

Its presence was inescapable. I could feel it pressing against me from all sides, invading my thoughts, my memories. It was no longer just a reflection of me—it had become something more, something **inhuman**, something born of the mirror world itself. It was everywhere, spreading through the shattered pieces of reality like a virus, infecting everything it touched.

I screamed, but no sound escaped my lips. There was no sound here, only the overwhelming silence of the void, broken only by the occasional, distant whispers of the doppelgänger's voice, echoing through my mind like a twisted mantra.

"You can't hide from me," it whispered, the words slithering through my thoughts like poison. "You've already become part of me. There's no escape."

I fell for what felt like an eternity, tumbling through that endless void of broken glass and shifting shadows. My mind was fracturing, splintering under the weight of it all. I couldn't tell where I ended and the mirror world began. Time had lost all meaning, and I was no longer sure if I was still myself or just another piece of the mirror's twisted reality.

Then, with a sudden, violent **jolt**, I hit the ground.

The impact knocked the breath from my lungs, leaving me gasping for air as I lay there, dazed and disoriented. The world around me spun in a dizzying blur, the edges of my vision flickering with strange lights and distorted shapes. For a moment, I couldn't move—couldn't think. I was completely overwhelmed, trapped in the overwhelming sensory chaos of the mirror world.

Slowly, painfully, I forced myself to sit up, my body trembling with the effort. The ground beneath me was cold and hard, the surface smooth like polished glass. I blinked, trying to clear the fog from my vision, and when the world finally came into focus, I realized where I was.

I had landed in the **mirror world**.

It wasn't like before—not the warped version of my home that I had seen the first time I crossed into this place. This was something far worse, far more **alien**. The landscape stretched out before me, vast and infinite, made entirely of broken, jagged shards of glass that reflected the twisted sky above. The sky itself was a sickly, swirling mass of colors—pale blues and greens and purples that shifted and churned like storm clouds.

And within those clouds, I saw **shapes**—vague, monstrous forms that moved just beyond the reach of comprehension, their outlines too vast, too impossible to grasp.

The air was thick with the same oppressive weight I had felt before, but here, it was far more suffocating. Every breath I took felt like I was inhaling cold smoke, filling my lungs with something foul and unnatural. The world around me pulsed with a strange energy, as though the very fabric of reality was alive, breathing in tandem with my own ragged breaths.

And then I heard it—the faint, steady **footsteps**.

I scrambled to my feet, my heart pounding in my chest as I looked around frantically, searching for the source of the sound. But I already knew what I would find.

The **doppelgänger**.

It was there, standing just a few feet away, its twisted form silhouetted against the shifting sky. It was even more grotesque than before—its body elongated, its limbs unnaturally long and thin, its head cocked at an odd angle, as though it were mocking me. Its face was a warped reflection of my own, but distorted, stretched into something monstrous. Its eyes were empty black voids, and its mouth was twisted into a wide, toothy grin that split its face almost in half.

"You've finally arrived," it whispered, its voice cold and mocking, echoing through the stillness of the mirror world. "Welcome to your new reality."

I backed away, my pulse racing, but the doppelgänger didn't move. It simply stood there, watching me with those empty eyes, its grin never faltering.

"What do you want from me?" I choked out, my voice trembling.

The doppelgänger tilted its head, as though considering the question. Then, slowly, it began to move toward me, its movements jerky and unnatural, like a puppet controlled by invisible strings.

"What do I want?" it repeated, its voice low and dangerous. "I want what was always meant to be mine."

I took another step back, my heart pounding in my chest. "I'm not yours! I'm not—"

"You're already mine," it hissed, cutting me off. "You've been mine since the moment you touched the mirror. You let me in, and now I've taken **everything**."

Its words hit me like a punch to the gut, knocking the air from my lungs. I stumbled backward, shaking my head in denial, but deep down, I knew it was telling the truth. I could feel its presence inside me, could feel the way it had wormed its way into my mind, twisting my thoughts, my memories, my very sense of self.

I had let it in. I had let it become part of me.

But I wasn't ready to give up—not yet.

"I'm still here," I said, my voice trembling but defiant. "You haven't won. You're just... just a reflection. You're not real."

The doppelgänger's grin widened, and it let out a soft, mocking laugh. "Oh, but I **am** real. I'm more real than you are. I'm what you've always been hiding from—what you've always feared becoming."

It stepped closer, and I could feel its cold presence pressing against me, suffocating me. "You can't fight me. You are me. You've always been me."

"No," I whispered, my voice barely audible.

The doppelgänger reached out, its long, skeletal fingers brushing against my skin, and I felt a cold shock of pain run through my body. It wasn't just physical pain—it was something deeper, something that cut through to my very soul. I could feel it draining me, pulling me into its twisted reality, into the mirror world where it ruled.

I stumbled back, gasping for breath, but the doppelgänger didn't stop. It moved closer, its presence overwhelming, and I could feel myself slipping, losing control, becoming part of it.

"You can't escape," it whispered, its voice low and seductive. "You've always been part of me. Let go."

My vision blurred, the world around me spinning as the doppelgänger's presence consumed me. I could feel it invading my mind, twisting my thoughts, turning everything I knew into something dark, something alien. I was losing myself, becoming part of the mirror, part of the thing that had always been waiting for me.

But then, in the depths of my mind, I heard another voice. **My voice.**

It was faint, but it was there—a small, fragile part of me that hadn't been consumed, that hadn't been twisted by the mirror world.

"Fight," it whispered.

With a surge of desperation, I reached for that voice, clinging to it with everything I had left. I couldn't let the doppelgänger win. I couldn't let it take me. Not completely.

I pushed back.

The doppelgänger recoiled, its grin faltering for the first time. I could feel its presence weakening, just slightly, but enough to give me a sliver of hope. I wasn't gone. Not yet.

I stepped forward, my hands trembling but steady. "You're not me," I whispered, my voice stronger now. "You'll never be me."

The doppelgänger snarled, its eyes burning with fury. "I am everything you are," it hissed. "You can't fight me forever."

"Maybe not," I said. "But I'm not giving up."

I reached out, my hand trembling, and placed it against the doppelgänger's chest.

The world shattered around us.

Chapter 15: The Reflection's Revenge

The world around me shattered in a burst of light and sound.

For a moment, everything was chaos—jagged shards of reality spinning around us like broken glass caught in a hurricane. The mirror world crumbled, its twisted landscape collapsing in on itself as the doppelgänger's grip faltered. The swirling sky fractured, the monstrous shapes within it dissolving into nothingness. And then, all at once, it was **silent**.

I fell to my knees, gasping for breath. My entire body trembled with exhaustion, the weight of what had just happened pressing down on me like a boulder. My mind was a blur of scattered thoughts and emotions, the line between reality and the mirror world still too blurred to make sense of. But I could feel it—I had won, if only for a moment.

The doppelgänger had recoiled. I had pushed back, found a piece of myself it hadn't been able to take. That small victory burned inside me like a fragile flame, flickering against the overwhelming darkness that still surrounded me.

I wasn't free yet.

I slowly raised my head, my eyes scanning the shattered remnants of the mirror world. The ground beneath me was cracked, jagged shards of glass embedded in the earth like teeth. The swirling colors of the sky had faded, replaced by a deep, suffocating blackness that seemed to press in from all sides.

And there, standing in the midst of the destruction, was the **doppelgänger**.

THE SPACE BETWEEN THE MIRROR

It hadn't disappeared. It hadn't crumbled with the mirror world. If anything, it had grown stronger—its twisted form taller, more imposing, with its limbs stretching in grotesque proportions. Its face, still a grotesque parody of my own, was contorted with fury, its mouth stretched into a snarl, revealing rows of jagged teeth that hadn't been there before.

"You think this is over?" it hissed, its voice dripping with venom. "You think you can fight me? You've only delayed the inevitable."

I stumbled to my feet, my legs weak beneath me, but I forced myself to stand. I couldn't let it see my fear. I couldn't let it know how close I was to breaking.

"I'm still here," I said, my voice shaky but defiant. "You haven't won."

The doppelgänger's snarl deepened, its eyes—those terrible, empty black voids—boring into me with a malevolent intensity. It took a step forward, its body rippling with unnatural movements, its limbs bending in ways that defied logic.

"You're **nothing**," it spat. "You're just a hollow shell, a reflection of something that was never real to begin with. You are **me**. You always have been."

Its words twisted through my mind, echoing in the corners of my thoughts, but I pushed them away. I couldn't let it get inside my head again. I had to stay focused, had to remember who I was, even if that identity felt fragile, even if the doppelgänger's words gnawed at the edges of my sense of self.

"I'm not you," I said through gritted teeth. "I'll never be you."

The doppelgänger laughed—a horrible, grating sound that seemed to reverberate through the very air around us. Its grin widened, its eyes gleaming with a sick, twisted amusement.

"You still don't understand, do you?" it whispered. "You can't fight me. I'm inside you. I'm part of you. Every time you've looked into a mirror, every time you've doubted yourself, I've been there. You can't separate yourself from me, because **you are me**."

I shook my head, backing away as the doppelgänger advanced, its voice growing louder, more insistent.

"You can't hide from your reflection," it said, its tone mocking. "You can't escape who you really are. Every fear you've ever had, every dark thought, every moment of weakness—that's **me**. I am everything you've tried to bury. And now I'm taking what's mine."

I was cornered. There was nowhere left to run, nowhere to hide. The jagged shards of glass that littered the ground surrounded me, cutting off any escape. The doppelgänger loomed over me, its twisted body casting long, grotesque shadows across the fractured landscape.

My mind raced. I could feel the mirror world pulling at me again, its cold tendrils wrapping around my thoughts, trying to drag me back into the darkness. The doppelgänger's words burrowed into my consciousness, making me doubt, making me question everything.

What if it was right? What if I really was just a reflection, a hollow imitation of something that had never truly existed? What if I had never been in control at all, and the doppelgänger had always been the real me?

But then, through the fog of fear and doubt, I remembered something—the moment I had pushed back, the moment I had **fought**. The doppelgänger had recoiled then. It had hesitated. It had **feared** me.

It wasn't invincible. It wasn't unbeatable.

It was a reflection. Just a reflection.

And reflections could be **broken**.

Summoning every last ounce of strength I had, I stood my ground, my fists clenched at my sides. The doppelgänger stopped, its twisted grin faltering as it sensed the shift in me.

"I'm not afraid of you," I said, my voice low but steady.

The doppelgänger's eyes narrowed, its body rippling with anger. "You should be," it hissed.

I shook my head, a strange calm settling over me. "You're just a reflection. You're not real. You're nothing without me."

For the first time, the doppelgänger hesitated. Its form wavered, flickering like a dying flame, and I saw something shift in its expression—something like uncertainty.

I stepped forward, my voice growing stronger. "You've been feeding on my fear, on my doubts. But I'm still here. I'm still **me**."

The doppelgänger snarled, its body distorting violently as it tried to reassert its dominance. "You can't win! You're mine! You've always been mine!"

"No," I said, my voice calm. "You're nothing without me."

I reached out, and for the first time, it was the doppelgänger that recoiled. Its body flickered, its form blurring as though it were struggling to maintain its shape. Its eyes—those terrible black voids—were wide with rage, but beneath that, I saw something else.

Fear.

It was afraid.

I took another step forward, my heart pounding in my chest but my mind clearer than it had been in a long time.

"You're nothing," I repeated, my voice steady. "And I'm not afraid of you anymore."

The doppelgänger let out a scream—a high-pitched, inhuman sound that shook the very ground beneath us. Its body convulsed, its limbs stretching and warping as it tried to pull itself back together, tried to hold on to the power it had over me. But it was too late. I had seen the truth.

It was just a reflection.

I lunged forward, my hand reaching for the doppelgänger's chest, and as my fingers touched its skin, I felt a strange, powerful surge of energy. The doppelgänger screamed again, its form flickering wildly as though it were being torn apart from the inside. Its twisted face contorted in agony, and for a moment, I saw flashes of myself—my real self—reflected in its eyes.

And then, with a final, shattering scream, the doppelgänger **broke**.

Its body dissolved into a swirling mass of dark, empty shards, the fragments of its form scattering into the air like dust. The mirror world around me trembled, the ground splitting apart as the doppelgänger's influence crumbled. The sky above me darkened, the monstrous shapes within it fading into the void, and I could feel the weight of the mirror world lifting, its grip on me finally loosening.

I fell to my knees, gasping for breath, my entire body trembling with exhaustion. The shattered pieces of the doppelgänger's form drifted through the air, dissolving into nothingness as they fell.

It was over.

I had won.

But as I knelt there, staring at the ground, I couldn't shake the feeling that something was still wrong. The mirror world was collapsing around me, dissolving into the darkness, but I could feel something—some small, lingering presence—still there.

And then I saw it.

In one of the jagged shards of glass that littered the ground, I saw a reflection.

It was **me**.

But it wasn't.

It was a fragment of the doppelgänger, a small, fractured piece that had survived. It stared up at me from the shard of glass, its eyes still wide with fury, its mouth twisted into a silent scream.

It was still there.

A part of it would always be there.

Waiting.

Chapter 16: The Last Door

The jagged shard of glass lay at my feet, reflecting the small fragment of the doppelgänger that had survived. Its twisted face, frozen in a silent scream of fury, stared back at me from the glass, reminding me that no matter how much I had fought, some part of it still remained. A small, lingering presence that refused to fade entirely.

I knelt down, my breath steadying as I studied the shard. The reflection felt distant now, like an echo of a nightmare, but it was still there, just under the surface. I reached out, hesitating for a moment, before my fingers brushed the cool, broken edge. I could feel its faint pull, like a dull throb in the back of my mind, the last remnant of the mirror world's influence. I lifted the shard slowly, turning it over in my hand, watching as the distorted reflection of the doppelgänger's face shimmered across the cracked surface.

It hadn't won. I knew that now. But it hadn't disappeared, either.

Something deep inside me told me this was how it would always be—a piece of that mirror world, a piece of **it**, would always remain. I had fought, I had broken the mirror's grip on me, but some things, once unleashed, couldn't be completely destroyed. I could sense the mirror world's presence still lingering at the edges of my perception, faint but undeniable, like a shadow that never truly fades.

I dropped the shard, letting it fall back to the ground with a soft clink, and stood, wiping the sweat from my brow. The mirror world around me had almost completely dissolved now, the once-fragmented landscape collapsing into a formless void. The sky was gone, the strange, alien architecture had crumbled, and the oppressive weight of the doppelgänger's presence had lifted.

But I still wasn't free. Not yet.

There was one last door.

It stood in the distance, a dark, looming shape at the very edge of the remaining fragments of the mirror world. Unlike the other doors I had encountered, this one was different. It was massive, its frame impossibly tall and wide, stretching up into the void like some monolithic structure that had been there for centuries. The door was made of ancient wood, scarred and blackened, with iron hinges that groaned under their own weight. There were no markings, no symbols, just a solid, imposing barrier between me and whatever lay beyond.

I knew, instinctively, that this was the final door. The door that would lead me out—back to my world, back to reality.

But I also knew that crossing through it wouldn't be easy.

I could feel it even from where I stood, the faint hum of energy that radiated from the door, the way it seemed to pulse in time with my heartbeat. It wasn't just a door—it was the last remnant of the mirror world, a final barrier that I would have to break through in order to truly escape.

I took a deep breath and began walking toward it, each step heavy with the weight of what I had endured. My mind still buzzed with fragments of memory, echoes of the doppelgänger's voice whispering in the corners of my consciousness. I could feel my identity, my sense of self, still fragile, still uncertain. But I had come too far to stop now. I had to push through.

As I approached the door, the air around me grew colder, denser, and I could feel the pressure building. The remnants of the mirror world clung to me like a second skin, its presence a constant reminder that this reality was not my own. But I pressed on, my hand reaching out toward the iron handle of the door.

The moment my fingers touched the cold metal, I felt it—a surge of energy, a deep, resonant hum that vibrated through my bones. The door wasn't just a passage; it was alive. It was the heart of the mirror world, the source of everything I had experienced, everything I had fought. It was the gateway between the two realities, and passing through it would either free me or consume me.

I hesitated, my fingers trembling against the iron handle. The weight of the decision pressed down on me, the fear of what might be waiting on the other side gnawing at the edges of my resolve. What if I wasn't ready? What if, after everything, the doppelgänger had left something inside me that would pull me back, that would drag me into the mirror world forever?

I could feel the doppelgänger's presence in the air around me, faint but there. It hadn't completely disappeared—it had simply receded, biding its time. And though I had fought it off, I knew that a part of it would always remain, lurking in the dark corners of my mind, waiting for a moment of weakness.

But I couldn't let that stop me. I had to move forward. I had to find my way back to the world I knew.

With a deep breath, I gripped the iron handle tightly and pulled.

The door creaked open slowly, the sound echoing through the vast emptiness of the mirror world. Cold air rushed through the gap, and I felt a shiver run down my spine as I peered into the darkness beyond. For a moment, there was nothing—just an endless black void, silent and still.

And then, from deep within the void, I heard it—a faint whisper, barely audible, like the soft rustle of leaves in the wind.

It was the doppelgänger.

"You'll never escape," it whispered, the words crawling through my mind like a virus. "I'm always with you. Always."

I clenched my jaw, fighting against the fear that gripped my heart. The doppelgänger was wrong. I had fought it once, and I would fight it again, if I had to. I wasn't going to let it control me, not anymore.

I stepped through the door.

The darkness closed around me like a blanket, swallowing me whole. For a brief, terrifying moment, I felt as though I were falling again, tumbling through the endless void of the mirror world, lost and helpless. But then, just as suddenly, the ground solidified beneath my feet, and the darkness lifted.

I was standing in my living room.

The air was warm and still, the soft glow of morning light filtering through the curtains. The familiar scent of home washed over me, and for a moment, I simply stood there, breathing it in, trying to ground myself in the reality of the moment. My heart still pounded in my chest, but the weight of the mirror world had lifted, replaced by the quiet calm of the real world.

I looked around, half-expecting to see some trace of the nightmare I had just endured, but there was nothing. The room was as it had always been—quiet, peaceful, untouched by the horrors I had faced. It was as if the mirror world had never existed.

But I knew better.

I walked over to the corner of the room where the mirror had once stood, my pulse quickening as I remembered the day I had brought it into my home. The spot was empty now, the mirror gone, shattered into a thousand pieces in the depths of the mirror world. And yet, as I stared at the empty space, I couldn't shake the feeling that something still lingered.

The mirror was gone, but its influence remained.

I walked over to the window and looked out at the quiet street below. The world outside looked normal—cars passing by, people walking their dogs, the sun shining down on the sidewalks. But I could feel it, deep in the pit of my stomach—a small, nagging presence that wouldn't leave.

The mirror world hadn't let me go completely. I had crossed through the door, but a part of it had crossed with me.

I turned away from the window, my mind heavy with the weight of what I had endured. I knew that, even though I had escaped, the mirror world would always be with me. It would be there in the reflections I passed, in the shadows that flickered at the edges of my vision. The doppelgänger was gone, but it had left a scar—a scar that would never fully heal.

And in the quiet of my home, I heard the faintest whisper.

"I'm always with you."

Chapter 17: Haunted by Reflections

The days after my return from the mirror world passed in a blur of quiet normalcy, but normal had taken on a new meaning. Nothing felt the same anymore. The familiar rhythm of my life had been disrupted by something far more insidious, something I couldn't quite shake. The doppelgänger had left its mark on me, and even though I had crossed through that final door back into my world, I couldn't rid myself of the feeling that I hadn't returned alone.

I tried to settle back into my life. Tried to convince myself that it was over. But the scar of the mirror world, of that terrible place with its warped reflections and monstrous beings, had sunk deep into my mind. I could feel it there, like a splinter buried under my skin. Every reflection I passed, every shadow that flickered in the corner of my vision, reminded me of what I had experienced.

And then, there were the **whispers**.

It started as a faint, barely audible sound—just a low hum in the background of my thoughts, easily brushed off as the aftereffects of trauma. But over time, the whispers grew louder, more insistent, until they became impossible to ignore. I could hear them in the stillness of my house, in the silence of the night, always just on the edge of perception. A voice—my voice, but not quite my own—echoing in the back of my mind, telling me things I didn't want to hear.

"You think it's over," the voice whispered, cold and mocking. "You think you escaped. But you didn't. You can't."

I shook my head, pressing my hands to my temples, trying to drown out the sound. But the voice was relentless, worming its way into my thoughts, twisting them, making me doubt myself, my reality.

"You let me in," it hissed. "And now I'm part of you. Forever."

I tried to ignore it. Tried to convince myself that it wasn't real. That it was just the remnants of the trauma I had endured, my mind playing tricks on me. But deep down, I knew the truth. The doppelgänger hadn't been destroyed. Not completely. A part of it had followed me back into my world, embedding itself in the fabric of my mind, feeding on my fear, my doubt.

It had been weeks since I'd returned, and in that time, I had done everything I could to avoid looking into mirrors, into any kind of reflection. It wasn't difficult at first—I removed the mirrors from my home, covered the reflective surfaces I couldn't get rid of. But reflections were everywhere. In windows, in pools of water, in the gleam of metal. I couldn't escape them. I couldn't escape **it**.

One night, after another restless day spent trying to ignore the whispers, I found myself staring out the window of my living room. The moon hung low in the sky, casting a pale, sickly light across the street below. The reflection of the room behind me shimmered faintly in the glass, distorted slightly by the imperfections in the windowpane.

And there, in the reflection, I saw **it**.

At first, it was just a flicker, a shadow that didn't belong. But as I stared, my heart pounding in my chest, the shadow took shape, solidifying into a figure—tall, thin, and wrong. Its face, or what passed for a face, was featureless at first, just a blur of darkness. But then, slowly, painfully, the features sharpened, and I saw **myself** staring back at me.

Not just my reflection.

The **doppelgänger**.

Its eyes locked onto mine, and that same terrible, mocking grin spread across its face, the corners of its mouth stretching too wide, too far, as though its skin were about to tear. The sight of it sent a cold wave of nausea crashing through me, and I stumbled back from the window, my breath catching in my throat.

But it didn't go away. The reflection remained, standing just inside the glass, watching me with those cold, empty eyes.

"I told you," it whispered, though its lips didn't move. The voice came from everywhere and nowhere, wrapping around me like a noose. "You can't escape me. I'm part of you now."

I backed away, my heart racing, the familiar surge of panic rising in my chest. This couldn't be happening. I had destroyed the mirror. I had crossed through the final door. I was free. But as I stared at the doppelgänger, its twisted reflection standing in the window, I realized that I had never truly escaped. It had followed me, woven itself into the very fabric of my reality.

And it wasn't going to stop.

I turned and ran, the weight of the doppelgänger's presence pressing down on me like a suffocating fog. The house seemed smaller, the walls closer, the shadows darker. Everywhere I turned, I felt it watching, waiting, always just out of sight, always just beyond the edge of my perception.

I fled into the kitchen, my hands shaking as I gripped the edge of the counter. I couldn't breathe, couldn't think. The voice was still there, hissing in my mind, laughing at my fear, my helplessness.

"You can't run," it whispered. "You can't hide."

I squeezed my eyes shut, trying to block it out, trying to hold on to what little sanity I had left. But the doppelgänger's voice was like a knife, cutting through my thoughts, slicing away at my sense of self.

"Just let go," it said softly, almost soothing. "Stop fighting. You've lost. You know you've lost."

I opened my eyes, my gaze darting to the kitchen window. The reflection was there too, waiting for me. The doppelgänger, still grinning, its eyes gleaming with a dark, malevolent light. My breath caught in my throat as I saw it move—**not in the window**, but behind me, in the reflection of the kitchen. It wasn't just in the glass. It was here, in the room with me.

Slowly, I turned around, my heart pounding in my chest.

The kitchen was empty.

But I could feel it.

It was **here**. Somewhere. Watching. Waiting.

And in the silence of the kitchen, I heard the faintest whisper.

"I'm always with you."

I stumbled back, my body trembling with fear. I couldn't escape it. It was inside me, inside my mind. I could feel it there, twisting my thoughts, distorting my perception of reality. No matter how far I ran, no matter how hard I tried to fight it, the doppelgänger would always be there, lurking in the shadows, in the reflections.

There was no escape.

I grabbed a knife from the counter, my hand shaking violently as I held it in front of me. Maybe I could fight it, maybe I could cut it out, sever the connection, end this nightmare once and for all.

But as I stood there, the cold steel trembling in my grip, I saw the reflection in the blade.

The **doppelgänger**, grinning.

"You think that will save you?" it whispered, its voice low and mocking. "You think you can cut me out? You can't cut out what's already part of you."

I dropped the knife, my body shaking with uncontrollable fear. The blade clattered to the floor, the sound sharp and jarring in the silence of the kitchen.

I was losing myself. I could feel it. The doppelgänger's influence was spreading through me, like a slow, creeping infection. Every thought, every emotion, felt tainted by its presence. My own reflection had become an enemy, a twisted reminder of the thing that had followed me back from the mirror world.

"I'm not afraid of you," I whispered, though my voice trembled with fear.

The doppelgänger's grin widened.

"Liar."

Chapter 18: Into the Dark Corners

I was running out of options, but more than that, I was running out of time. The doppelgänger's whispers had become a constant hum in my mind, its voice winding through every thought, every moment. It was no longer just a part of me; it was **inside** me, burrowing deeper with every passing hour. There was nowhere to escape, nowhere to hide. Every reflective surface, every dark corner, seemed to hold its presence, waiting for the moment when I would finally break.

I sat in the dim light of my living room, the curtains drawn tight to keep the outside world at bay, though I knew it wouldn't help. The house was silent, but the silence felt oppressive, thick with the weight of the unseen. I hadn't looked into a mirror in days, hadn't dared to catch my reflection in anything, but it didn't matter. The doppelgänger didn't need mirrors anymore.

I could feel it everywhere.

"You're slipping," it whispered in my mind, its voice like cold fingers trailing down my spine. "You can't hold on much longer."

I closed my eyes, pressing my palms to my temples in a desperate attempt to block it out, but the voice only grew louder, more insistent.

"You can't keep fighting me. I'm part of you now."

The fear gnawed at me, hollowing me out from the inside. How long had it been since I crossed back from the mirror world? Weeks? Months? Time had lost all meaning. Every day felt the same, a slow descent into madness, with the doppelgänger lurking in every shadow, every corner of my mind. I couldn't tell where I ended and where it began anymore.

I opened my eyes and scanned the room. The reflections were everywhere—small, subtle, but always there. The gleam of the polished wooden floor, the faint shimmer on the glass of the picture frames, the faint outline of myself in the darkened television screen. I had tried to ignore them, tried to convince myself that they were harmless, but I knew better now. The doppelgänger was waiting in every one of them, watching me through the glass.

Waiting.

I stood abruptly, my pulse racing, my heart pounding in my chest. I couldn't stay here. I had to **do something**, anything to break free of this nightmare. Sitting still, doing nothing, only gave it more power, more control over me. I had to act. I had to find a way to stop it, to sever the connection before it consumed me entirely.

But how?

"You can't," the voice whispered, soft and cold. "You're mine."

I shook my head, trying to silence it, but the whispers slithered deeper into my mind.

"There's nowhere left to run," it said, mockingly. "You opened the door, remember? You let me in."

I staggered back, my breath catching in my throat. The memories of that first moment—the moment I touched the mirror—flooded my mind, a vivid rush of fear and confusion. I had let it in. I had been curious, reckless, and now I was paying the price.

But was that the only way in? Was the mirror the only connection, or had I made a mistake much earlier?

My thoughts raced back to that night—the night I had first noticed the subtle change in my reflection, the night I had been drawn to the mirror like something was pulling me toward it. What if the mirror had only been the beginning? What if something else, something far deeper, had allowed the doppelgänger to take root in my life, in my mind?

I needed answers.

With trembling hands, I fumbled through the mess of papers and notebooks I had scattered across the coffee table in a desperate search for some kind of clue, something I had missed in the chaos of my descent into the mirror world. There had to be **something**—some connection, some explanation that I hadn't seen before.

Then I found it.

Buried beneath the clutter of papers was an old journal, the worn leather cover cracked and faded. It had been mine for years, though I hadn't touched it in what felt like forever. I had forgotten about it entirely. But as I opened it, flipping through the yellowed pages, I realized that it had been there all along—the **warning signs**, the subtle shifts in my perception, the moments when the reflection had first begun to change.

I had written about it, though I barely remembered doing so. Pages filled with vague descriptions of dreams I couldn't fully recall, strange feelings of being watched, and odd flashes of myself in the mirror that didn't quite seem right. At first, I had dismissed it as stress, exhaustion. But it had been happening for far longer than I realized. Long before I had touched the mirror.

THE SPACE BETWEEN THE MIRROR

The doppelgänger had been there from the beginning, lurking in the dark corners of my mind, waiting for its moment.

And now, it had **me**.

As I read through the journal, my stomach twisted with dread. I could see it clearly now, the slow unraveling of my own mind, the way the doppelgänger had quietly slipped into my thoughts, into my life, without me even noticing. I had been losing control long before the mirror appeared. The mirror had only **accelerated** the process.

I dropped the journal, my hands shaking. The whispers had grown louder, more urgent, filling my mind with a cacophony of voices, all blending together into one suffocating presence.

"See?" the doppelgänger whispered, its voice wrapping around me like a noose. "You were always mine. I've always been here."

I stumbled back, my vision blurring as the room seemed to warp around me. The shadows on the walls stretched and twisted, growing darker, deeper. The reflection in the window flickered, the faint outline of the doppelgänger's face appearing once again, its grin wide and malicious.

"You let me in," it whispered, the words echoing in my skull. "You let me **become you**."

I couldn't take it anymore. The fear, the whispers, the constant pressure—it was too much. I had to stop it. I had to end this, somehow, before I lost myself completely.

I turned toward the door, my mind racing. There had to be a way to fight it, to sever the connection once and for all. I couldn't let it win. I wouldn't.

But as I reached for the door, something strange happened.

The shadows in the room shifted, swirling around me like a living thing. The air grew cold, heavy, and I could feel the presence of the doppelgänger pressing down on me from all sides, suffocating me with its dark, malevolent energy.

And then, as if from the depths of my own mind, a **new voice** spoke. Not the doppelgänger's, but something else. Something far more ancient, far more powerful.

"You are not the first," it said, the words low and rumbling, like the grinding of stone. "And you will not be the last."

I froze, my heart pounding in my chest. The voice was everywhere and nowhere, filling the room, filling my thoughts. It wasn't the doppelgänger. It was something else. Something **older**.

"You opened the door," the voice continued, "but you did not understand what you were inviting in."

My breath caught in my throat as the realization hit me. The mirror. The doppelgänger. It wasn't just an isolated event. It was part of something much bigger, something I had unknowingly stumbled into. There were **others**. Others like me who had touched the mirror, who had let something in. And whatever I had unleashed was only a small part of it.

"What are you?" I whispered, my voice trembling.

The shadows seemed to pulse around me, the air thick with the presence of whatever was speaking. I could feel its ancient power pressing down on me, its voice resonating through the walls, through my very bones.

"I am the reflection of all who have come before," the voice said. "I am the mirror of your darkest self. I am what you feared most. And now, I am **you**."

The words sent a jolt of terror through me, but before I could react, the shadows surged forward, enveloping me in darkness.

Chapter 19: The Revelation of Shadows

I was swallowed by the shadows. Their cold embrace wrapped around me, suffocating and vast, pulling me down into an abyss I couldn't comprehend. The doppelgänger's presence clung to me, a constant whisper in my mind, but now it was joined by something older, something far more terrifying. It wasn't just a reflection. It wasn't just a distorted version of me. It was something far deeper—**a force that had always been there**.

I felt as though I were falling again, tumbling through the dark void, the weight of the unknown pressing against my chest. My breath was shallow, each gasp of air tinged with panic. The voice, ancient and deep, echoed through the darkness, a low rumble that resonated in my bones.

"You have opened the door to your darkest self," it said. "And now, the shadows will claim you."

I struggled to hold on to reality, to keep some semblance of myself intact as the shadows seemed to pull at the edges of my mind, unravelling everything I thought I knew. The memories of the mirror world, of the doppelgänger, flooded through me, but now they were overlaid with something darker. The mirrors hadn't just shown me a distorted reflection. They had opened a door to a truth I wasn't ready to face—a truth that had been waiting in the shadows all along.

"You thought the doppelgänger was the end," the voice whispered, its tone almost mocking. "But the mirror was just the beginning."

THE SPACE BETWEEN THE MIRROR 93

I couldn't see anything around me, but I could feel it—**the presence**, ancient and relentless, surrounding me, pressing into my thoughts. My mind was a battlefield, my identity torn apart piece by piece. I wasn't just fighting the doppelgänger anymore. I was fighting the very essence of the mirror world itself.

The shadows shifted, and out of the void, I saw shapes begin to form. Tall, thin figures, their limbs too long, their faces featureless and smooth—**the Eyeless Figures**. They were here, just as they had been in the mirror world, moving slowly toward me, their heads tilted as though listening to something I couldn't hear. They seemed to glide through the air, their movements silent, their presence overwhelming.

I backed away, my body trembling, but there was nowhere to run. The void surrounded me, infinite and dark, and the Eyeless Figures closed in from all sides. Their faceless heads turned toward me, and I could feel their attention—an almost palpable force pressing against my mind. It was as though they were studying me, examining me, as if I were some kind of specimen they had been waiting to claim.

And then I saw **it**.

At the center of the figures, something else began to emerge from the darkness—**a shape**, twisted and grotesque, pulling itself from the void like a nightmare crawling out of the depths of the subconscious. It was tall, its body bent at unnatural angles, its limbs stretching and writhing as though they were made of smoke. But the most horrifying part was its face.

It was **me**.

Not the doppelgänger, not a reflection, but something worse—an image of myself that had been warped beyond recognition, its features twisted into something monstrous. Its eyes were empty voids, its skin stretched tight across its skull, its mouth a gaping black hole that seemed to swallow all light. As it moved toward me, I could feel the immense **weight** of its presence, like a storm bearing down on me, crushing me under its force.

"You are not who you think you are," the voice said, its words cutting through the darkness like a blade. "You have never been in control."

The monstrous version of me stopped just in front of me, its empty eyes staring into mine, and for a moment, I couldn't breathe. I was frozen, unable to move, unable to look away from the horror in front of me.

"This is your true self," the voice whispered. "This is what you have been hiding from all along. The reflection was only a shadow of the truth."

I stumbled back, my legs weak beneath me, but the figure didn't move. It simply stood there, watching me with those dark, empty eyes, its mouth hanging open in a silent scream. The Eyeless Figures moved closer, their presence surrounding me, and I felt the suffocating weight of the mirror world pressing in from all sides.

I had thought the doppelgänger was my greatest fear, my greatest enemy. But I had been wrong.

The doppelgänger had only been a mirror of what I was becoming—this was the **truth**. The mirror world wasn't just a reflection of my darkest self—it was a reflection of **everything I had hidden**, everything I had refused to face.

"You are part of the mirror world now," the voice said, its tone final, absolute. "You have always been."

The figure in front of me moved suddenly, its limbs jerking violently as it reached for me, its long, twisted fingers stretching out like claws. I tried to back away, but my body wouldn't respond. I was paralyzed, trapped in the grip of the shadows, unable to escape.

The figure's hand touched my chest, and the moment it did, I felt a surge of cold, unbearable pain shoot through me. It wasn't just physical pain—it was something deeper, something that reached into the core of my being and tore me apart from the inside.

I screamed, the sound ripped from my throat as the figure's hand sank deeper into my chest. I could feel it **pulling** at something inside me, something essential, something that had always been there but that I had never fully understood.

"You are one of us," the voice whispered. "You have always been one of us."

I could feel myself slipping, my mind unraveling, the last threads of my identity being torn away. The shadows swirled around me, pulling me down into the darkness, and I knew that if I didn't do something—**anything**—I would be lost forever. The mirror world would claim me completely, and there would be no escape.

With a surge of desperation, I reached out, grabbing the figure's wrist with both hands. Its skin was cold and slick, like wet stone, and I could feel the immense power pulsing beneath its surface. But I held on, refusing to let it consume me.

"No," I gasped, my voice barely a whisper. "I won't... let you..."

The figure's grip tightened, its hand sinking deeper, and for a moment, I thought it was over. But then, something strange happened. The cold that had been seeping into me—into my mind, my soul—suddenly stopped. The pressure eased, just slightly, and I could feel a faint flicker of **resistance** deep inside me.

I focused on that flicker, clinging to it with everything I had left. I wasn't going to let this thing take me. I wasn't going to let the mirror world claim me. Not like this.

"I am... **not**... you," I said through gritted teeth, forcing the words out.

The figure let out a low, guttural growl, its grip tightening once again, but I could feel its power wavering. I could feel the darkness around me shifting, the weight of the shadows lifting ever so slightly.

"I am not one of you!" I screamed, summoning every ounce of strength I had.

The figure let out a terrible, inhuman scream, its body convulsing violently as it recoiled, pulling its hand from my chest. The shadows around me exploded outward, the Eyeless Figures retreating into the void as the ancient presence that had surrounded me began to weaken.

I collapsed to the ground, gasping for breath, my body trembling with exhaustion. The void around me was still there, but it was fading, dissolving into nothingness. The monstrous figure—the warped version of myself—was gone, its presence scattered into the darkness.

I was alone again.

The voice, the ancient presence that had spoken to me, was silent.

But as I lay there, staring into the vast emptiness of the void, I knew the truth.

I had won, but not completely. The mirror world would never truly let me go. It had marked me, claimed a part of me that I could never take back. I had fought off the darkness, but the shadows would always be there, lurking at the edges of my mind, waiting for the moment when I would slip again.

And in that moment, when I was weakest, they would return.

Chapter 20: A World of Mirrors

The void that had surrounded me moments ago began to dissolve, fading like mist in the morning light. I remained on the ground, gasping for breath, my body trembling with exhaustion. The encounter with the monstrous version of myself had left me drained, but not broken. I had fought back, pushed away the darkness. Yet, as I lay there, staring into the vast nothingness that surrounded me, I knew I was far from free.

The ancient presence that had spoken to me was silent now, but its words lingered in my mind, echoing in the dark corners of my thoughts: *You have always been one of us.*

I forced myself to stand, my legs shaking beneath me. The darkness around me continued to recede, revealing glimpses of something beyond the void—a world, familiar yet distorted. As the shadows peeled away, I realized where I was.

It was my house.

But it wasn't the same.

The living room stretched out before me, but it had been transformed. The walls, the furniture, the very air—everything had taken on a glossy, reflective sheen, as though the entire space had been submerged in glass. It wasn't just the room that had changed. The house felt **bigger**, its dimensions warped, extending beyond what was physically possible.

And then I understood.

I was still in the **mirror world**.

The door I had passed through hadn't taken me back to reality. It had only brought me deeper into the labyrinth of reflections, deeper into the nightmare that had been waiting for me all along. The mirror world had reshaped itself, becoming a twisted, infinite version of my home, filled with impossible spaces and distorted reflections.

I looked around, my heart sinking as the realization settled over me. Everywhere I turned, there were reflections—on the walls, on the floor, on the ceiling. Countless versions of myself stared back at me from every surface, some warped, some perfect, but all of them watching me with cold, unblinking eyes. It was as though I had stepped into a hall of mirrors, a place where I could never escape my own image, where I could never escape **myself**.

A surge of panic rose in my chest, my breath coming in short, ragged gasps. I couldn't stay here. I couldn't stay trapped in this endless reflection, surrounded by versions of myself, each one a reminder of the doppelgänger that still lurked in the shadows.

I turned toward the hallway, my eyes scanning for an exit, but the space seemed to stretch on forever, the walls shifting and bending in ways that defied logic. No matter how far I walked, the end of the hallway never came. The doors that lined the walls were all mirrors—each one reflecting a version of me, each one a potential trap waiting to pull me deeper into the mirror world.

"You can't leave," a voice whispered, soft and insidious.

I froze, my heart pounding in my chest.

It was the doppelgänger.

I hadn't seen it since the battle in the void, but I could feel its presence. It hadn't been destroyed, not completely. I knew that now. It had simply been waiting, biding its time, waiting for the moment when I would let my guard down.

"You're still mine," it whispered, its voice echoing from every reflection. "You'll always be mine."

I swallowed hard, my pulse racing as I spun around, searching for the source of the voice. But the reflections were everywhere, stretching out in all directions, and no matter where I looked, I saw nothing but my own image staring back at me.

"This world belongs to me," the voice continued. "And now, so do you."

I couldn't take it anymore. I couldn't stand the constant barrage of reflections, the endless reminders of the thing that had followed me from the mirror world. My mind was unraveling, pulled in too many directions at once, each version of me a twisted reflection of the fear that gripped my heart.

"I'm not yours," I whispered, though my voice trembled with uncertainty.

The doppelgänger's laugh echoed through the space, a low, mocking sound that sent a shiver down my spine.

"You still don't understand," it said, its tone cold and sharp. "This isn't about control. It's about **acceptance**."

I took a step back, my heart racing as the reflections around me shimmered and shifted. The versions of me in the mirrors began to change, their faces twisting and warping into grotesque parodies of myself—some with hollow eyes, others with too-wide grins, all of them watching, waiting.

"You've spent your whole life running from the truth," the doppelgänger whispered, its voice weaving through the air like smoke. "You've been hiding, pretending to be something you're not. But you can't run anymore."

The mirrors surrounding me began to tremble, their surfaces rippling as though disturbed by some unseen force. I could feel the weight of the doppelgänger's presence pressing down on me, suffocating me, pulling me deeper into the endless reflection.

"You can't escape what you are," the doppelgänger hissed. "You're part of this world now."

I stumbled back, my vision blurring as the walls seemed to close in around me. The mirrors loomed larger, their surfaces warping and distorting, and in every one, I saw a different version of myself—each one more monstrous than the last.

The reflections began to **move**.

One by one, they stepped out of the mirrors, their twisted forms pulling themselves free from the glass like specters emerging from the depths of a dark pool. I watched in horror as they surrounded me, their hollow eyes fixed on mine, their mouths twisted into hideous grins.

"You can't hide from yourself," the doppelgänger whispered.

The reflections moved closer, their bodies shifting and contorting as they reached for me, their hands long and skeletal, their fingers claw-like. I backed away, my breath coming in shallow gasps as I searched for an escape, but there was none. The mirrors stretched on forever, the reflections multiplying with every step I took, until I was surrounded by a sea of distorted versions of myself.

"You can't run," the voice said, growing louder, more insistent. "You can't fight this. You're already mine."

I felt their cold hands touch my skin, their fingers curling around my arms, my shoulders, pulling me down into the abyss of reflections. I screamed, thrashing against their grip, but it was no use. They were too many. I was outnumbered, overwhelmed.

The doppelgänger stepped forward from the shadows, its face a perfect reflection of mine, but its eyes—those dark, empty voids—were filled with triumph. It knelt before me, its hand reaching out to touch my face.

"You've been fighting for so long," it whispered. "But it's over now. You're home."

I struggled, tears burning in my eyes as I tried to break free, but the doppelgänger's touch was cold and final. I could feel it draining the last of my strength, the last of my will to resist.

The reflections closed in around me, their hollow eyes shining with a dark, malevolent light. They were **me**, and I was them. I couldn't tell where I ended and they began anymore. The mirror world had claimed me.

And then, just as the darkness began to swallow me whole, something changed.

In the distance, at the farthest edge of the mirrors, I saw a flicker of light—a faint, pulsing glow that cut through the endless reflections like a beacon.

Hope.

It was small, barely visible, but it was there. A way out.

I summoned every last bit of strength I had left, pushing against the reflections, against the doppelgänger's cold grip, and **I ran**.

The mirrors shattered around me, their surfaces exploding into shards of glass as I broke free from their grasp. The

THE SPACE BETWEEN THE MIRROR

doppelgänger's scream echoed through the air, a sound of pure, primal rage, but I didn't stop. I ran toward the light, toward the one thing that might save me from the nightmare that had consumed my life.

The light grew brighter, and as I reached out to touch it, I felt the weight of the mirror world lift from my shoulders. The reflections disappeared, the doppelgänger's voice fading into nothingness, and for the first time in what felt like an eternity, I was **free**.

The light enveloped me, pulling me out of the dark, distorted world of mirrors and into something new. Something real.

When the light faded, I found myself standing in a quiet, sunlit room. My room. The walls were solid, the floor beneath my feet firm. There were no reflections, no mirrors. Just the soft, warm glow of morning light filtering through the window.

I collapsed to the floor, tears streaming down my face.

I had made it. I had escaped.

But even as I lay there, gasping for breath, I knew the truth.

The mirror world was still out there, waiting. The doppelgänger hadn't been destroyed. It had only been pushed back. And one day, when the shadows grew long and the light faded, it would return.

But for now, I was free.

For now.

Chapter 21: A Fragile Peace

For days after my escape, I lived in a haze. The world around me had returned to normal—or at least, it appeared to. The oppressive weight of the mirror world was gone, and the doppelgänger no longer haunted every shadow. But the relief I felt was fragile, tenuous. It was as though my mind had been stretched too far, and now, in the quiet moments, I could feel it fraying at the edges.

I avoided mirrors entirely. I covered the bathroom mirror, removed every reflective surface from my house, and avoided looking into windows or any surface that might cast back my image. I couldn't bear to see my reflection—not because I feared the doppelgänger would return, but because I no longer trusted that the face staring back at me would be **mine**.

There was a new silence in my home now, a kind of emptiness that followed me from room to room. Even in broad daylight, I found myself glancing over my shoulder, half expecting to see something lurking just behind me, hiding in the corner of my vision. But every time I turned, there was nothing. No reflections. No twisted versions of myself. Just the stillness of my house, bathed in the soft glow of sunlight.

I had escaped the mirror world, but it hadn't left me. I could feel its presence lingering, like a faint, invisible weight pressing down on my chest. It wasn't gone—not completely. It was waiting, watching, biding its time.

But there was something else that gnawed at the edges of my mind, something that haunted me even more than the memory of the doppelgänger.

The **light**.

I couldn't shake the memory of that light—the small, flickering beacon that had saved me from the mirror world's grasp. It had appeared when I was at my lowest, when I had been moments away from losing myself completely. But where had it come from? What was it?

And more importantly, why did I feel like it had been a **warning**?

Days passed, and I began to notice small, unsettling changes. At first, they were subtle—shadows that seemed to shift when I wasn't looking, the sound of faint whispers just beyond my hearing, an unsettling sense that I wasn't alone even when I knew I was. I chalked it up to the trauma of everything I had been through. My mind was still fragile, still recovering from the horrors of the mirror world. But as the days stretched into weeks, the changes became harder to ignore.

One night, as I lay in bed, trying to force myself into the oblivion of sleep, I heard it again.

The **whisper**.

It was faint at first, barely noticeable, like the distant sound of wind rustling through the trees. But as I lay there, my heart racing, it grew louder, more distinct. It wasn't the doppelgänger's voice—this was something different. Something **older**.

I sat up, my pulse pounding in my ears, and strained to listen. The whisper seemed to be coming from somewhere deep within the house, carried on a breeze that shouldn't have existed. I climbed out of bed, my feet hitting the cold floor, and followed the sound, my body trembling with a mixture of fear and anticipation.

The whisper led me to the hallway—the same hallway that had once stretched on forever in the mirror world. But now, it was just a hallway, ordinary and mundane, its walls bathed in the soft glow of the nightlight I had plugged in weeks ago. The whisper grew louder as I approached the end of the hallway, and there, at the far end, I saw something that made my blood run cold.

A **mirror**.

It was small, no bigger than a picture frame, propped against the wall as though it had been placed there deliberately. I knew it hadn't been there before—I had removed every mirror from the house. I had been **certain** of it. But now, here it was, gleaming faintly in the dim light, casting back a distorted reflection of the hallway.

I stopped in my tracks, my heart hammering in my chest. The whisper had stopped now, replaced by a heavy, oppressive silence that filled the hallway. My eyes were locked on the mirror, every instinct in my body screaming at me to turn away, to **run**.

But I couldn't. I had to know.

I stepped closer, my breath shallow, my hands trembling at my sides. The reflection in the mirror shifted as I moved, but there was something wrong with it—something **off**. It wasn't just the distortion of the glass; it was something deeper, something that lurked beneath the surface of the reflection.

I knelt down in front of the mirror, my breath catching in my throat as I stared into its depths. At first, I saw nothing but my own face staring back at me—pale, wide-eyed, and filled with fear. But then, slowly, the reflection began to change.

The walls in the reflection seemed to stretch, elongating into impossible angles, just as they had in the mirror world. The hallway behind me warped and twisted, its dimensions bending and folding in on themselves, until the reflection no longer resembled the reality I knew. And then, from deep within the reflection, I saw it.

A **shadow**, moving at the farthest edge of the mirror.

I froze, my breath catching in my throat, my pulse pounding in my ears. The shadow was faint, barely visible at first, but as I stared into the mirror, it began to take shape. It was tall, thin, its form shifting and rippling as though it were made of smoke.

And then, as the shadow drew closer, I saw its face.

It was **me**.

Not the doppelgänger. Not a twisted, monstrous version of myself. It was me, exactly as I appeared now—tired, broken, afraid. The figure in the mirror moved closer, its eyes locked onto mine, and for a brief moment, I felt a surge of something I hadn't felt in a long time.

Recognition.

The figure knelt in front of the mirror, its face inches from mine, its eyes filled with a quiet sadness. It didn't smile, didn't speak. It simply stared at me, and in that moment, I understood.

This was the truth. The real truth that the mirror world had been trying to show me all along.

The reflection wasn't an enemy. It wasn't a monster. It was **me**—the part of me I had been running from, the part of me I had refused to face. The mirror world hadn't been trying to claim me. It had been trying to **reveal** me.

I reached out, my hand trembling, and touched the surface of the mirror. The glass was cool beneath my fingertips, and as I made contact, the reflection shimmered, rippling like water disturbed by a stone.

The figure in the mirror mirrored my movements, reaching out with its own hand until our fingertips touched. The moment we made contact, I felt a surge of energy—warm, familiar, and strangely comforting.

The figure smiled then, a small, sad smile, and I felt the weight that had been pressing down on me for so long begin to lift. The mirror world, the doppelgänger, the shadows—they had all been leading me to this moment, forcing me to confront the parts of myself I had been too afraid to face.

The reflection wasn't my enemy.

It was my **truth**.

I pulled my hand away from the mirror, and as I did, the reflection faded, dissolving into the dim light of the hallway. The mirror remained, silent and still, its surface smooth and unbroken.

I stood there for a long time, staring at the mirror, feeling the weight of everything that had happened slowly begin to lift. The mirror world was still there, waiting, but it no longer felt like a threat. It felt like a reminder—a reminder that I couldn't run from myself, no matter how far I tried to go.

The whispers were gone now, replaced by a quiet, fragile peace. I knew the mirror world would always be there, lurking at the edges of my mind, waiting for the moment when I would look into the glass again. But I no longer feared it.

I had faced my reflection, and for the first time, I had understood.

I turned away from the mirror and walked back to my bedroom, my steps slow but steady. The house was quiet, the oppressive weight that had once filled the air now gone. As I climbed into bed, pulling the blankets around me, I felt a strange sense of calm settle over me.

The mirror world hadn't claimed me. Not completely. But it had changed me. I would never be the same, and in some ways, I was grateful for that. I had seen the darkest parts of myself, and I had survived.

And as I drifted off to sleep, I heard a faint whisper, not of warning, but of quiet understanding.

"You are home."

Chapter 22: The Deepening Shadows

The days following my return to a tentative normalcy were filled with an odd quiet. Though I had faced my reflection, accepted the parts of myself I had once feared, I couldn't shake the feeling that something was still watching, still lurking in the corners of my vision. Every time I thought I'd escaped the mirror world, it would find some subtle way to remind me it was still there, its influence stretching just beyond the threshold of reality.

I had banished the doppelgänger—or so I thought—but now, in the stillness of my home, I wondered if I had only postponed the inevitable. The doppelgänger hadn't shown itself in days, but the feeling of its presence, the weight of its existence, was ever-present. It didn't need to speak anymore; it was always with me, lingering like a shadow.

I avoided mirrors, reflective surfaces, anything that might pull me back into that nightmare world. I covered every mirror in the house with cloth, unwilling to confront the possibility of the mirror world reasserting its control. Yet, I couldn't escape the feeling that this was only a temporary reprieve. The mirror world was not something that could be defeated—it was too vast, too **ancient**. I had merely scratched the surface.

I had come to understand that much.

As the days passed, I began to notice subtle changes in the house. The light would flicker at odd times, casting long, unnatural shadows. Sometimes, the sound of my footsteps would echo just a little too long, as though there was

THE SPACE BETWEEN THE MIRROR

something else moving alongside me. The feeling of being watched grew stronger with each passing day, and the whispering I had heard in the mirror world began to creep back into the edges of my hearing.

The peace I had found was unraveling, fraying at the seams. I knew it wouldn't last.

One evening, after a particularly unsettling day, I found myself standing in front of the mirror I had covered in the hallway. I hadn't intended to confront it, hadn't wanted to. But something had pulled me toward it. A kind of compulsion, a quiet voice in the back of my mind urging me to **look**.

I stared at the cloth draped over the mirror, my breath shallow. My hands trembled as I reached for the edge of the fabric, my heart pounding in my chest. I knew that looking into the mirror would invite something back into my life—something dark and insidious—but I couldn't stop myself.

The house felt too quiet. The air was too still. It was as though the very walls were holding their breath, waiting for me to make a move.

With a deep breath, I pulled the cloth away.

The mirror shimmered in the dim light of the hallway, reflecting the walls and the soft glow of the nightlight. I hesitated, waiting for something to happen, expecting the reflection to shift, to change into something terrible. But it didn't. The mirror remained still, its surface calm and unbroken.

And yet, as I stared into it, I felt the familiar weight of the mirror world pressing against the edges of my perception. It was there, just beyond the glass, waiting for me. It hadn't gone anywhere—it had simply been waiting for me to make the first move.

I leaned in closer, my breath fogging the surface of the glass. My reflection stared back at me, but this time, it wasn't twisted or distorted. It was **me**, as I was—tired, uncertain, afraid. I searched the reflection for any sign of the doppelgänger, any hint of the darkness that had once consumed me, but there was nothing. The reflection was still.

But that stillness was unsettling.

Then, from deep within the mirror, I heard it.

A **whisper**.

It was faint, barely audible, but unmistakable. The same whisper I had heard in the mirror world. The same whisper that had haunted me in the darkest moments of my descent. It slithered through the air like a snake, coiling around my thoughts, pulling me closer to the glass.

I pressed my hand against the surface of the mirror, and as I did, the whisper grew louder.

"You're still here," it said, the voice soft and insistent. "You never left."

I pulled my hand away, stumbling back, my pulse racing. The mirror's surface rippled, just for a moment, as though something beneath it had shifted. The whisper faded, replaced by a cold, suffocating silence that filled the hallway.

I stared at the mirror, my mind racing. The reflection was gone now, replaced by a faint, shimmering outline of my form. It was as though the mirror had erased me, wiped me from its surface entirely.

I took a step back, my heart pounding. I knew what this meant. The mirror world wasn't done with me. I hadn't escaped. Not truly. It had let me go because it knew I would return. Because it knew I couldn't resist its pull.

And then I heard the whisper again, this time from the depths of my own mind.

"You can't hide from the truth."

I turned and ran. I didn't care where I was going; I just had to get away from the mirror, from the suffocating weight of its presence. I sprinted down the hallway, my feet pounding against the floor, my breath coming in short, panicked gasps. But no matter how far I ran, I couldn't escape the feeling that the mirror world was closing in around me, pulling me back into its depths.

I reached the living room, collapsing onto the couch, my body trembling with fear. The house was dark now, the only light coming from the flickering glow of the nightlight in the hallway. My mind raced, trying to make sense of what had just happened, trying to understand the meaning of the whisper.

The mirror world hadn't let me go because I had won.

It had let me go because it knew that I could never escape.

I buried my face in my hands, my breath ragged, the weight of the realization crashing down on me like a tidal wave. I had fought so hard to reclaim my life, to rid myself of the doppelgänger and the horrors of the mirror world, but in the end, it had been for nothing.

The mirror world was a part of me now.

It had always been.

And as I sat there, the whisper returned, soft and insistent, wrapping itself around my thoughts like a noose.

"You belong to us."

I lifted my head, staring into the darkness of the living room. The whisper was louder now, more demanding. The weight of the mirror world pressed down on me, suffocating, inescapable. I could feel it tightening its grip, pulling me back toward the glass, back toward the place I had fought so hard to escape.

I closed my eyes, trying to block out the sound, trying to drown out the voice that was now a constant presence in my mind.

But it wouldn't stop.

The mirror world wouldn't stop.

And deep down, I knew the truth.

I would never be free.

Chapter 23: The Thin Veil

I tried to settle back into the quiet of my home, but the mirror world had followed me, its tendrils wrapped tightly around my reality. The sensation that something was always watching lingered in every room, hiding in the smallest reflections, waiting for me to look too long into the glass. The sense of peace I had briefly found after confronting the mirror was crumbling. I couldn't deny it any longer: the mirror world had never truly let go.

Each night, as the hours crept into the deep darkness, the veil between my world and the mirror world seemed to grow thinner. The strange occurrences became more frequent, more invasive. At first, they were small things—objects slightly out of place, shadows moving where no light could cast them, the faint sound of my own voice whispering in the distance.

But now, the occurrences were becoming **impossible to ignore**.

One night, as I lay in bed, I heard something unmistakable—the slow creak of a door opening somewhere in the house. My breath hitched, and I sat up in bed, every muscle in my body tense. I listened, my heart thudding loudly in my chest. The house was silent, but the air was thick with the feeling that something was moving, something **unseen**.

I climbed out of bed, my feet hitting the cold floor with a soft thud. Every instinct in my body told me to stay put, to pretend that nothing had happened, but I couldn't. I had to know.

I moved quietly down the hallway, the same hallway where the mirror had first shown its true face. The creaking sound came again, and this time, I knew where it was coming from.

The **living room**.

I hesitated at the threshold of the room, my hand resting on the frame of the door. The darkness inside the living room was absolute, thicker than it should have been, as though the shadows themselves were **waiting**. I reached out and flicked on the light switch.

The light flickered once, twice, and then stayed on.

Everything in the living room appeared exactly as it should, nothing out of place. But the feeling that something was wrong hung heavily in the air, like a storm waiting to break. I took a slow step into the room, my breath shallow, my skin prickling with tension. I scanned every corner, every inch of the space, looking for something—anything—that would explain the eerie sensation of being watched.

Then, I noticed it.

The small, round **mirror** on the wall near the window. I had forgotten to cover it.

I felt my stomach twist with dread. I had been so careful to cover every reflective surface, but this one had slipped through. It was small, inconspicuous, a decorative piece I rarely even noticed, but now it loomed large in the dim light of the room.

As I moved closer, I could see my reflection in the glass—my pale, wide-eyed face staring back at me, my expression mirroring the fear I felt. But there was something else in the reflection, something that made my heart pound in my chest.

THE SPACE BETWEEN THE MIRROR   117

Behind me, in the reflection, I saw the **door** that led to the hallway slowly swinging open.

I spun around, my breath catching in my throat, but the door was closed. I stared at it for a long moment, my mind racing to make sense of what I had just seen. Slowly, I turned back to the mirror.

The door was still open in the reflection.

A cold wave of nausea washed over me. This wasn't possible. The door was closed—I could see it, I could feel it. But in the mirror, the door stood open, and beyond it, the hallway stretched out into darkness, impossibly long, far longer than it should have been.

I took a step back, my heart racing, my pulse pounding in my ears. The mirror world was breaking through again, twisting reality, bending the rules of space and time. The thin veil between our worlds was **tearing**, and I could feel it pulling at the edges of my mind.

Suddenly, a soft creaking sound filled the room again, and I turned to the door once more. It was still closed, but in the reflection, I saw it open wider. The darkness beyond it deepened, and I could sense something moving in the shadows—something just out of sight.

My breath caught in my throat as I watched the darkness in the reflection shift and swirl, like smoke rising from a fire. The air in the room grew colder, and I could feel the presence of the mirror world pressing down on me, suffocating, as though the walls themselves were closing in.

Then, from the depths of the reflection, I saw **movement**.

At first, it was just a flicker, a shadow in the distance. But as I watched, it grew closer, taking shape. A figure, tall and thin, its limbs too long, its body swaying unnaturally as it moved. It stepped out of the dark hallway in the reflection, and my heart lurched in my chest as I recognized the figure.

It was **me**.

Not the doppelgänger, not the twisted version of myself that had haunted me in the mirror world—but me, exactly as I was now. The figure moved slowly, deliberately, its eyes—my eyes—locked onto mine through the glass. There was no malice in its gaze, no mockery. Just cold, quiet understanding.

I stumbled back, my mind reeling, my body trembling with fear. I didn't understand what I was seeing. I didn't know if it was the mirror world pulling me in again or if this was something else—something worse.

The reflection of myself in the mirror raised its hand, as though beckoning me closer, its expression unreadable. I stood frozen, my breath shallow, my body refusing to move.

And then, the figure spoke.

Its voice was soft, almost a whisper, but I heard it clearly.

"It's time."

The words sent a jolt of terror through me, and I stumbled back, nearly tripping over the edge of the couch. I stared at the reflection, my heart pounding in my chest. The figure—the **me** in the mirror—remained still, its hand still raised, its eyes fixed on mine.

"It's time," it repeated, its voice calm, certain.

I shook my head, my pulse racing. Time for what? What was it trying to tell me?

The reflection didn't move, didn't speak again. It just stood there, waiting, its presence filling the room, suffocating me with the weight of the truth I didn't want to face.

THE SPACE BETWEEN THE MIRROR

The door in the reflection opened wider, the darkness beyond it yawning like an abyss. I could feel it now—the pull of the mirror world, stronger than ever before, dragging me toward the glass, toward the other side.

I stepped back, my body trembling, but I couldn't tear my eyes away from the reflection. The figure—myself—beckoned again, and I felt the familiar, irresistible urge to **follow**.

I knew, deep down, that this was the moment I had been dreading. The moment when the mirror world would demand something from me, something I couldn't refuse.

"It's time," the reflection whispered one last time.

With a final, trembling breath, I stepped forward.

The air around me shifted, the world tilting as the pull of the mirror world grew stronger, more insistent. The glass rippled beneath my touch, and I felt the familiar cold embrace of the other side waiting for me.

I closed my eyes and stepped through.

Chapter 24: The Crossing

The moment I stepped through the mirror, the world around me dissolved. The cold, familiar weight of the mirror world enveloped me, pulling me into its depths. I could feel the reality I had known slipping away, like sand falling through my fingers, until there was nothing left but the hollow, suffocating presence of the other side.

I blinked, disoriented, my breath catching in my throat as I tried to regain my bearings. The air was thick and cold, filled with a sense of dread that seemed to cling to my skin. The space around me wasn't the chaotic, fractured version of my home I had once encountered. This place was different—silent, still, and vast, like an endless void.

I stood in darkness, but it wasn't the oppressive blackness I had feared. It was a deeper, stranger kind of dark—one that felt alive, as though the shadows themselves were watching, waiting for me to make my next move. The ground beneath my feet was smooth and cold, like polished glass, and as I looked down, I saw my reflection staring back at me from the floor.

It was **me**—but something was wrong. The reflection didn't move with me. It stood still, staring up at me with a hollow, emotionless gaze. I felt a chill run down my spine as I knelt to touch the glassy surface, my fingers trembling. The moment I made contact, the reflection smiled.

I stumbled back, my heart racing.

"You made the choice," a voice said from behind me.

I turned sharply, my pulse pounding in my ears, and there, standing just a few feet away, was the figure I had seen in the mirror. It was **me**, but not the twisted doppelgänger I had once feared. This version of me was calm, composed, its face serene and unreadable. It stood with its arms crossed, watching me with quiet intensity, as though it had been waiting for this moment.

"It's time to stop running," it said, its voice steady. "You knew you couldn't avoid this forever."

My breath caught in my throat as I stared at the figure. This wasn't the same entity that had hunted me through the mirror world, but there was something unsettling in its eyes—something that felt too knowing, too familiar.

"What are you?" I whispered.

The figure smiled softly. "You already know the answer."

I took a step back, my mind racing. The mirror world had always been a reflection of my own mind, my fears, my doubts. But this—this felt different. It wasn't a reflection of my darkness, but of something deeper, something I hadn't yet faced.

"I'm not like you," I said, my voice trembling. "I won't let the mirror world take me."

The figure tilted its head slightly, as though considering my words. "The mirror world doesn't want to take you. It wants to show you the truth."

My pulse quickened. "What truth?"

The figure's expression softened. "The truth you've been running from all this time. The truth about who you really are."

I shook my head, stepping further back, the smooth surface of the ground reflecting every movement. "I've seen the truth. I faced it. I accepted it."

The figure let out a small, almost sad laugh. "You've only accepted part of it. The part you were willing to see. But there's more."

The air around me seemed to grow colder, heavier, and I could feel the weight of the mirror world pressing down on me, pulling at the edges of my mind. The figure stepped closer, its eyes locked on mine, and I felt the familiar pull of the other side, the same pull that had drawn me through the mirror in the first place.

"You've been afraid," the figure continued. "Afraid of what the mirror might show you. Afraid of what you might find on the other side. But fear has kept you blind."

I swallowed hard, trying to push down the rising tide of panic. The figure was right—I had been running. I had spent so long avoiding my reflection, fearing what it might reveal, that I hadn't allowed myself to truly see.

"What is it you want me to see?" I asked, my voice barely a whisper.

The figure reached out, its hand hovering just above my shoulder. "It's not about what I want. It's about what you've been hiding."

I felt a surge of emotion rise in my chest—fear, anger, confusion—all of it swirling together in a chaotic storm. I didn't understand what the figure was trying to tell me, didn't understand why the mirror world had called me back. But deep down, I knew there was something I hadn't confronted, something buried deep within me.

"I don't understand," I said, shaking my head.

The figure sighed softly, as though it had expected my response. "You've seen fragments of yourself in the mirror world. The doppelgänger, the shadows, the whispers. They're all pieces of you—pieces you've refused to acknowledge."

I stared at the figure, my breath coming in shallow gasps. "What do you mean?"

The figure's eyes softened, filled with a quiet sadness. "The mirror world doesn't create anything. It only reflects what's already there."

My heart pounded in my chest as the weight of the words sank in. The mirror world wasn't an outside force, wasn't something separate from me. It was a reflection of **me**—of everything I had been running from, everything I had refused to face.

The figure stepped closer, its voice gentle but firm. "You've been afraid of your own reflection because you've been afraid of what it might reveal. But you can't run from yourself forever."

I swallowed hard, the air in my lungs tight and heavy. The figure was right—I had been running. I had spent so long hiding from my reflection, from the parts of myself I didn't want to see, that I had trapped myself in a cycle of fear.

The mirror world wasn't the enemy. It was a mirror, showing me the truth I had refused to accept.

I took a deep, trembling breath and looked up at the figure. "What do I have to do?"

The figure smiled softly. "Stop running."

I felt the weight of those words settle over me, the truth of them sinking deep into my bones. I had been running for so long—running from the reflection, from the doppelgänger, from the mirror world itself. But now, standing here in the cold, still darkness, I understood.

I wasn't running from the mirror world.

I was running from **myself**.

I turned back to the ground beneath my feet, the smooth surface reflecting my image perfectly. The reflection no longer felt threatening. It felt familiar, like a part of me I had forgotten but was now ready to face.

The figure stood beside me, its presence comforting in a way I hadn't expected. "You can end this," it said. "But first, you have to stop fearing what you see."

I nodded slowly, the fear that had once gripped me loosening its hold. I knelt down and placed my hand on the smooth surface of the ground, my fingers brushing against the glassy reflection.

For the first time, I didn't flinch. I didn't pull away.

I faced the reflection—faced **myself**.

And in that moment, something changed.

The cold weight of the mirror world lifted, the darkness around me thinning. The reflection shifted, no longer a distortion of who I was, but a clear, honest image of **me**. The fear I had carried for so long melted away, replaced by a quiet understanding.

I had always been part of the mirror world, but I wasn't its prisoner. The reflection wasn't a trap—it was a guide, showing me the parts of myself I had been too afraid to see.

I stood, feeling lighter than I had in years, and turned to face the figure.

"I'm ready," I said.

The figure smiled, a soft, knowing smile. "Then it's time to go home."

The air around me shimmered, the mirror world dissolving into light, and I felt myself pulled back into the familiar

THE SPACE BETWEEN THE MIRROR

warmth of my reality. The weight of the reflection, the darkness, the fear—it all faded, leaving only a quiet sense of peace.

I opened my eyes to find myself standing in my living room, the small mirror on the wall reflecting the soft glow of the nightlight.

I was home.

And this time, I knew I wouldn't be running anymore.

Chapter 25: The Return of the Light

The peace I had found upon my return from the mirror world was unlike anything I had expected. After confronting my reflection, embracing the parts of myself I had spent so long running from, it felt as though a great weight had been lifted from my shoulders. The fear that had once consumed me was gone. For the first time in what felt like an eternity, I was able to live without the constant feeling that something was lurking in the shadows, waiting for me to falter.

The mirror in the hallway, once a source of dread, was now simply a mirror—no longer a doorway to some twisted version of reality, but a harmless object. I left it uncovered, no longer afraid of what I might see. Every time I passed by it, I saw myself, and nothing more. There was no whispering voice, no shifting shadows. Just the quiet, familiar reflection of my life.

Weeks passed, and my days were filled with an unexpected normalcy. I went about my routine, trying to rebuild the life that had been torn apart by the horrors of the mirror world. But even as I settled into this new sense of calm, there was a part of me that remained cautious, wary. I knew that the mirror world hadn't disappeared. It was still there, waiting, watching. But now, I understood its purpose. It wasn't a malevolent force—it was a reflection, a mirror of my own fears, my own doubts. And as long as I faced those parts of myself, I knew I could keep it at bay.

One evening, as the sun began to set, casting long shadows across the floor of my living room, I felt the first stirrings of unease. It wasn't the sharp, immediate fear I had felt before, but something subtler, a faint pull at the edge of my awareness. I stood in the kitchen, staring out the window as the sky shifted from pale blue to deep purple, and I felt it again—the sense that something was **changing**.

The air in the house seemed to grow heavier, and the light from the setting sun took on a strange, dim quality, as though it were being filtered through a veil of darkness. I turned away from the window and walked into the hallway, my pulse quickening as I approached the mirror. The reflection was still there, as normal as ever, but the feeling of unease grew stronger.

And then, I saw it.

At first, it was just a flicker, a faint shimmer of light at the edges of the mirror's surface. I blinked, unsure of what I was seeing. The light grew stronger, brighter, until it was unmistakable. It was the same light I had seen before—the one that had saved me in the depths of the mirror world.

My breath caught in my throat as I stepped closer to the mirror. The light pulsed gently, a soft, warm glow that filled the hallway with a strange, otherworldly radiance. It wasn't threatening, but it carried with it a sense of **urgency**, as though it were calling me, beckoning me toward something.

I reached out and touched the surface of the mirror, half expecting to be pulled back into the mirror world. But this time, the glass remained solid beneath my fingertips. The light flickered, growing brighter for a moment before dimming again. It was as though the mirror was trying to show me something, something I had missed.

I took a step back, my heart racing, and for the first time in weeks, I felt a familiar whisper at the edges of my mind. But it wasn't the cold, mocking voice of the doppelgänger. It was something different, something softer, more insistent.

"It's time."

The words sent a chill down my spine, but I wasn't afraid. Not anymore. I had faced the mirror world, faced the truth about myself, and I had survived. Whatever the mirror was trying to show me now, I was ready.

I stood before the mirror, waiting, my breath shallow as the light continued to pulse gently, almost as though it were alive. The room around me seemed to grow dimmer, the shadows lengthening as the light from the mirror grew brighter. I watched in silence as the reflection of the hallway began to fade, replaced by something else—something I had seen before.

The door.

It was the same door that had appeared in the mirror world, the one I had passed through to return to my reality. But this time, it didn't feel like a threat. The door was bathed in the soft, golden light, and it stood open, waiting for me.

I took a deep breath and stepped forward, my hand reaching for the surface of the mirror. The glass shimmered beneath my touch, and for a moment, I felt a familiar pull, the same pull I had felt when I first crossed into the mirror world. But this time, there was no fear. There was only a quiet sense of **acceptance**.

I pressed my hand harder against the glass, and the world around me dissolved into light.

For a moment, I was suspended in a warm, golden glow, the familiar sensation of weightlessness washing over me. I wasn't afraid. I knew, deep down, that this was where I was meant to

THE SPACE BETWEEN THE MIRROR

be. The mirror world hadn't called me back to trap me—it had called me to **show me something**.

When the light faded, I found myself standing in the mirror world once again, but this time, it was different. The chaotic, fractured landscape was gone. In its place was a vast, endless field of soft grass, stretching out in every direction under a sky filled with brilliant, golden light. The air was warm and still, and I could feel a sense of peace settling over me.

The mirrors that had once lined the landscape, reflecting twisted versions of reality, were nowhere to be seen. Instead, there was only the quiet, comforting presence of the light, filling the world with a sense of calm I had never known.

I walked forward, my steps slow and steady, the grass soft beneath my feet. There was no sense of urgency, no sense of dread. For the first time in as long as I could remember, I felt **free**.

And then I saw it.

In the distance, bathed in the warm glow of the light, stood the figure—the same figure I had seen before, the one that had guided me through the mirror world. It was **me**, but not a reflection. This version of me was whole, complete, unburdened by fear or doubt.

I approached the figure, my heart pounding in my chest, and as I drew closer, the figure smiled—a soft, knowing smile, filled with understanding.

"It's time," the figure said, its voice calm and steady.

I nodded, not needing to ask what it meant.

The mirror world had brought me here for a reason. It wasn't about fear, or danger, or being trapped. It was about finding peace, about embracing the parts of myself I had spent so long running from.

The figure stepped aside, revealing a small, simple mirror behind it. The glass was clear, unbroken, reflecting nothing but the soft light of the world around it.

"This is your choice," the figure said. "You can leave the mirror world behind, or you can stay."

I stared at the mirror, my mind racing. I had fought so hard to escape the mirror world, to reclaim my life. But now, standing here, I understood that the mirror world wasn't a prison. It was a place of reflection, of understanding. It had shown me the truth about myself, and now, it was offering me a choice.

I could leave. I could return to my world, my life, and move forward, unburdened by the fear that had once consumed me.

Or I could stay.

I reached out and touched the surface of the mirror, my hand trembling.

The light around me shimmered, and I felt the weight of the decision settle over me.

I took a deep breath, closed my eyes, and made my choice.

Chapter 26: The Other Side

I felt the cold surface of the mirror under my fingertips, the glass smooth and unyielding. The choice I had made was final, and yet, for a moment, I hesitated. The figure—my reflection, but also more than just that—stood silently beside me, watching, waiting for me to fully embrace my decision.

The light in the mirror world shimmered gently around us, casting long shadows that didn't seem threatening anymore. The air was still and peaceful, yet charged with a strange energy. I could feel it—this place was alive in a way that was hard to define. It was not just a reflection of my own inner world but something more—a place of understanding, of truths long hidden.

As I withdrew my hand from the mirror, the glass rippled once more, a soft wave of energy moving outward from where my fingertips had touched. The reflection wavered, then settled into an image that was so clear, so still, it felt like looking into a pool of perfectly calm water. But there was no reflection of me in the glass—only the soft golden light, now steady and inviting.

The figure—the other me—stepped forward, closer to the mirror. It moved with a calm, purposeful grace, not a reflection of my movements but an independent entity that I had come to recognize as part of me. This version of myself represented something I had spent so long avoiding: the part of me that was at peace, the part that no longer feared the mirror world or its revelations.

"You made the right choice," it said softly, its voice steady, filled with a quiet wisdom that seemed to come from somewhere deep within me.

I stared at the figure for a long moment, trying to understand what I was truly seeing. It wasn't the doppelgänger, nor was it just a reflection. It was something deeper—a manifestation of the acceptance I had fought so hard to reach.

"Are you... part of me?" I asked, my voice trembling slightly. I wasn't sure if I wanted to hear the answer.

The figure smiled—a gentle, reassuring smile that immediately calmed the anxiety rising in my chest. "Yes. I've always been part of you. But you've been afraid to see me, to acknowledge that I'm here."

I blinked, the weight of the words sinking in. All this time, I had been running from the truth—running from myself. The mirror world had reflected my fear back at me, showing me only what I had refused to accept. And now, here I was, standing face to face with the part of myself I had hidden away for so long.

I took a deep breath and asked the question I had been too afraid to ask: "What happens now?"

The figure tilted its head slightly, considering my words. "Now, you have a choice. You can return to the world you came from, the world where you spent so much time running from your reflection. Or you can stay here, in this place, and explore the truth that you've been shown."

I frowned, confused. "Stay here? But this place... it's the mirror world. It's not real."

The figure's expression softened. "Reality is not as fixed as you think. The mirror world is as real as you allow it to be. It's not a prison, not anymore. It's a place of reflection, of understanding. You've seen the darkness it can hold, but now you've seen the light too. This world can be whatever you make of it."

I looked around, taking in the vast, open landscape that stretched out before me. The grass swayed gently in the soft breeze, and the golden light bathed everything in a warm glow. There were no jagged edges, no dark shadows lurking at the edges of my vision. This wasn't the same mirror world that had terrified me before. It was something new, something filled with peace and possibility.

"You're saying I can choose to stay here?" I asked, my voice barely a whisper.

The figure nodded. "Yes. You've faced your fears, confronted the truth about yourself. You've accepted the reflection for what it is. Now, the choice is yours."

I stared at the mirror again, my mind racing. The decision felt monumental, far greater than anything I had ever faced. I could return to my world, to the life I had known before the mirror world had invaded it, or I could stay here, in this place of quiet reflection, where I had finally found a sense of peace.

But was this peace real? Was it something I could hold on to?

I turned back to the figure, my heart pounding. "If I stay here, what happens to the life I've built? The life I left behind?"

The figure's gaze didn't waver. "That life will continue without you. But this isn't about abandoning your old life. It's about choosing how you want to live now, with the truth you've discovered."

I swallowed hard, my throat dry. "And if I go back?"

"If you go back," the figure said softly, "you'll return with the knowledge you've gained here. You'll still carry the reflection with you, but it won't haunt you as it once did. You'll have faced it, and you'll know how to live alongside it."

I looked down at my hands, my fingers trembling slightly. The choice wasn't simple. I had finally found peace, finally faced the parts of myself I had been too afraid to acknowledge. But leaving behind the world I had known, the life I had fought so hard to reclaim—it felt like too great a sacrifice.

But going back... Would I fall into the same patterns? Would I lose this sense of clarity?

"I don't know what to do," I whispered.

The figure stepped closer, placing a hand gently on my shoulder. "You don't have to decide right now. The choice is yours, and it will remain yours as long as you need it to. But remember: this place isn't about running away. It's about understanding."

I nodded slowly, feeling the weight of the decision settle over me.

"I'll go back," I said, my voice quiet but resolute. "I'm not ready to stay here. Not yet."

The figure smiled again, a smile filled with understanding and acceptance. "That's your choice. And it's the right one for you."

I stepped forward, my hand once again brushing the surface of the mirror. The golden light shimmered, and I felt the familiar pull of the mirror world begin to release its hold on me.

"Will I see you again?" I asked, turning to look at the figure one last time.

"You'll always see me," it replied. "Because I'm part of you now. You'll carry this peace with you, no matter where you go."

I smiled faintly, feeling a warmth spread through my chest. The fear, the doubt, the darkness that had once consumed me—they were still there, but now they felt manageable, something I could live with, something I could understand.

The mirror shimmered one final time, and then the world dissolved into light.

I opened my eyes to find myself back in my living room, the soft hum of the night filling the quiet space. The mirror on the wall reflected the calm, still room, and as I looked into it, I saw myself—no longer afraid, no longer running.

I was home.

I smiled faintly, knowing that while the mirror world would always be with me, I had finally made peace with it. The reflection no longer felt like a threat. It felt like a part of me—a part I could live with.

For the first time in a long while, I felt truly **whole**.

Chapter 27: The Echoes of the Past

I thought returning to the real world would feel like stepping back into a place I knew well, but everything felt different. The house I had once feared was now calm, and the familiar objects of my life had taken on a new quality—less threatening, more grounded. Yet, as the days passed, I began to realize that the mirror world wasn't as far behind me as I had hoped. The reflections, though no longer filled with dread, still held a subtle power. They had become reminders, not of fear, but of something deeper, something unresolved.

At first, it was just a faint sense of being watched again. Not the oppressive, suffocating feeling that the doppelgänger had brought, but a presence, like the reflection of myself was always observing me, even when I wasn't near a mirror. It didn't feel malicious, but it didn't feel entirely benign either. It was as though a door had been opened, and while I had stepped back into my world, I couldn't close it completely.

One night, I sat on the couch in the quiet of the evening, the soft glow of a lamp casting long shadows across the room. The house was still, but the silence felt heavier than usual. I couldn't shake the feeling that something had shifted—something **new**, or perhaps **old**, had returned. It wasn't fear, but an unsettling recognition that my time in the mirror world had left marks on me, scars I couldn't yet see.

As I sat there, lost in thought, a soft sound broke through the stillness. It was a creak, almost imperceptible, coming from the hallway. I stood up, my heart skipping a beat, and walked slowly toward the sound.

THE SPACE BETWEEN THE MIRROR 137

The hallway was dim, illuminated only by the faint light from the living room. My eyes were drawn immediately to the mirror on the wall—the one that had shown me the door, the one that had once been the gateway to the mirror world. The mirror's surface was calm, reflecting the hallway and the soft shadows that clung to the walls.

I stared at it, waiting, unsure of what I was expecting to see. But there was nothing—no movement, no shifting shadows, no whispering voice. Just the quiet stillness of my home.

I turned away, letting out a slow breath. It was over. I had made my choice to return, and the mirror world had let me go. Whatever I was feeling now, it was just a residue of my time there—nothing more.

But as I walked back toward the living room, something stopped me in my tracks. It was faint, barely there, but unmistakable.

A **whisper**.

I froze, my pulse quickening, my eyes darting back toward the mirror. The whisper was faint, like a breath of wind through an open window, but it was there. And it was coming from the mirror.

I turned slowly, my heart pounding in my chest, and walked back toward the hallway. The mirror's surface remained unchanged, calm and still, but the whisper grew louder the closer I got. It was soft, almost imperceptible, but familiar. Too familiar.

I stepped in front of the mirror, my breath catching in my throat. The reflection showed nothing unusual—just the hallway behind me, stretching out in quiet stillness. But the whisper... it was louder now, clearer. And it was saying my name.

"Come closer," the voice said, so faint it was almost drowned by the silence.

I swallowed hard, my hands trembling at my sides. I knew that voice. It wasn't the doppelgänger. It wasn't the twisted reflection that had haunted me in the past. This voice was different.

It was **mine**.

I stepped closer to the mirror, my heart racing. The whisper continued, soft and insistent, urging me forward. I could feel the pull of the mirror world again, the same pull that had drawn me in before. But this time, it didn't feel like a trap. It felt like an invitation.

"Come closer," the voice repeated, more urgent now. "You need to see."

I pressed my hand against the surface of the mirror, half expecting it to ripple beneath my touch. But the glass remained solid, cool against my skin. The whisper grew louder, and for a moment, I thought I saw something—just a flicker of movement in the reflection. Something just beyond the edge of my vision.

I leaned in, my face inches from the glass, my breath fogging the surface.

And then I saw it.

At first, it was just a shadow—a faint outline in the background of the reflection. But as I stared, it took shape, becoming clearer, more defined.

It was **me**.

Not the calm, serene version of myself I had encountered in the mirror world, but the real me—standing there in the reflection, watching, waiting.

I took a step back, my heart racing. The reflection didn't move. It just stood there, staring back at me with a look of quiet intensity.

"Who are you?" I whispered, my voice trembling.

The reflection tilted its head slightly, its expression unreadable. "I'm you," it said softly. "But not the you that you know."

I swallowed hard, my mind reeling. "What do you mean?"

The reflection smiled—a sad, knowing smile. "I'm the part of you that you left behind. The part you've been trying to forget."

I shook my head, stepping further back from the mirror. "I don't understand."

The reflection's eyes softened. "You've been running from the truth for so long that you've forgotten what it feels like to be whole. You've confronted the mirror world, but you haven't confronted what brought you there in the first place."

I stared at the reflection, my breath coming in shallow gasps. "I thought I faced the truth. I thought I accepted it."

The reflection took a step forward in the glass, its hand reaching out as though it wanted to touch me. "You've accepted part of the truth. But there's more. You know there's more."

I felt a cold shiver run down my spine. The reflection was right. I had faced the fear of the mirror world, faced the darkness that had haunted me for so long. But there were still things I hadn't confronted—things I had buried deep inside, hoping they would never resurface.

"What do you want from me?" I asked, my voice barely a whisper.

The reflection smiled again, that same sad smile. "It's not about what I want. It's about what you need."

I swallowed hard, the weight of the words sinking in. I had thought my journey with the mirror world was over, but now I realized that it had only been the beginning. There were still parts of myself I hadn't faced, still shadows lurking in the corners of my mind, waiting to be brought into the light.

I stepped closer to the mirror again, my hand trembling as I reached out to touch the glass. The reflection watched me, its eyes filled with a quiet understanding.

"Are you ready?" it asked softly.

I took a deep breath, my heart pounding in my chest.

"Yes," I whispered. "I'm ready."

The reflection nodded, and in that moment, the surface of the mirror began to ripple, just as it had the first time I crossed into the mirror world. But this time, it didn't feel like I was being pulled into something dark and twisted. It felt like I was stepping into something familiar—something I had always known, but had been too afraid to face.

I pressed my hand harder against the glass, and the world around me dissolved into light.

Chapter 28: The Unveiling

The moment I stepped through the mirror, the world shifted again. But this time, it wasn't the chaotic, dark landscape of the mirror world that awaited me. Instead, I found myself standing in a room that looked almost exactly like my own living room. The same furniture, the same soft light filtering through the curtains, the same familiar smell of home. But something was different. There was an underlying strangeness to it all, as though I were looking at my life through a slightly distorted lens.

I turned in place, my pulse quickening as I took in the room. It was so eerily familiar, and yet... wrong. The edges of the room seemed to blur, like a dream that wasn't fully formed, and the air felt thicker, charged with something unseen.

My reflection stood beside me, no longer in the mirror, but right here, in the room. It moved with a calm certainty, as though it had always belonged here. It didn't look at me but instead scanned the room with the same intensity that I did.

"This is your past," it said quietly, its voice like a soft breeze rustling through a forest.

"My past?" I echoed, confused. I looked around again, trying to find some clue as to what the reflection meant. Everything seemed so normal, but as I moved deeper into the room, I realized that the objects around me weren't just everyday things. Each piece of furniture, each small object, held a significance I hadn't noticed before—memories, emotions, fragments of my life I hadn't confronted.

The reflection gestured toward a small table in the corner, where an old photo sat in a delicate frame. I walked over to it slowly, my heart thudding in my chest. I knew this photo well—it was a picture of me and my parents from when I was a child, a happy moment frozen in time. But as I stared at the photo, something shifted. The edges of the image blurred, and the people in the photo began to fade.

I gasped, stepping back, my hands shaking. "What's happening?"

The reflection stood behind me, its presence calm and unwavering. "This is what you've forgotten. What you've buried."

The photo continued to blur, the faces becoming indistinct, until only the outline of the figures remained. I could feel a deep ache in my chest, a pain I hadn't felt in years, rising to the surface. I had hidden these memories away for so long, locked them behind the walls of my mind. But now, here they were, unraveling before me.

I turned away from the photo, the room feeling smaller, more oppressive. "I don't want to remember this."

"You have to," the reflection said, stepping closer. "You came to the mirror world because you were running from your own life. You were running from the truth."

I swallowed hard, trying to push down the rising tide of emotion. "I've already faced my fears. I've confronted the mirror world. Why am I back here?"

The reflection's eyes softened. "Because you didn't face **everything**. You accepted part of yourself, but there are still things you're hiding from. And until you confront those, you'll never be truly free."

I felt a surge of frustration rise within me. "I don't understand. What do you want from me? What is the mirror world trying to show me?"

The reflection stepped in front of me, its gaze steady and filled with a deep sadness. "It's not about what the mirror world wants. It's about what you've been refusing to see."

I stared at the reflection, my mind racing. There was a part of me that understood, a part of me that knew exactly what the reflection was talking about. But I had spent so long burying those memories, so long pushing them aside, that the thought of confronting them now felt overwhelming.

"What is it that I've forgotten?" I whispered, my voice trembling.

The reflection didn't answer immediately. Instead, it turned toward the door at the far end of the room, the same door that had led me into the mirror world before. This time, however, the door wasn't dark or ominous. It glowed faintly, a soft light spilling out from beneath it, as though it was inviting me forward.

"You already know," the reflection said softly. "You've just been too afraid to look."

I hesitated for a moment, my heart pounding in my chest, before I took a step toward the door. The air in the room seemed to grow heavier with each step, the weight of my unspoken memories pressing down on me. But I couldn't turn back now. I had come too far.

As I reached for the door handle, my fingers trembling, I felt a cold rush of air wash over me. The light from the door flickered, and for a brief moment, I thought I heard a voice—a faint, distant whisper, just beyond the threshold.

I took a deep breath and pushed the door open.

On the other side, the world shifted again, and I found myself standing in a place I hadn't seen in years. It was the house I had grown up in, but it wasn't as I remembered it. The walls were faded, the furniture covered in dust, as though it had been abandoned for a long time. The air was thick with the smell of age, and the faint light from the windows cast long, distorted shadows across the floor.

I stepped inside, my heart heavy with a mixture of dread and sadness. Memories I had tried so hard to forget came rushing back, overwhelming me with their intensity. The laughter, the arguments, the quiet moments of loneliness—all of it was here, preserved in the walls of this place.

The reflection stood beside me, its presence a quiet comfort. "This is where it began," it said softly. "This is where you started running."

I walked through the rooms slowly, my hands brushing against the dusty furniture, my mind flooded with memories. I hadn't been back here in years, not since my parents had passed. I had shut the door on this part of my life, convinced that if I didn't look back, I could move forward. But now, standing here, I realized that I had never truly left this place behind.

"This is what you've been hiding from," the reflection said, its voice gentle. "Not the mirror world, not the doppelgänger. This."

I swallowed hard, tears burning in my eyes. "I didn't want to remember."

The reflection placed a hand on my shoulder, its touch light but steady. "You need to. You need to confront the things you've buried if you want to be free."

I closed my eyes, the weight of the memories almost too much to bear. I could see it all so clearly now—the moments of joy, the moments of pain, the loss that had shaped me into the person I had become. I had spent so long running from these feelings, convinced that if I ignored them, they would disappear. But now I understood that the mirror world hadn't just been about my fears—it had been about my past, my **truth**.

I opened my eyes, looking around the old house one last time. The dust, the faded walls, the lingering echoes of the past—they were all part of me. I had been running for so long, afraid to confront the pain, afraid to face the truth of who I was.

But now, I was ready.

I turned to the reflection, my voice steady despite the tears in my eyes. "I'm ready to stop running."

The reflection smiled, its expression filled with a quiet pride. "Then it's time to let go."

I took a deep breath, and for the first time in years, I allowed myself to feel the full weight of the memories—the loss, the pain, the love. It washed over me in waves, but I didn't resist it. I let it in, let it fill me, and then, slowly, I let it go.

The room around me began to fade, the old house dissolving into light, and I felt the weight lifting from my shoulders. The reflection stood beside me, its presence a quiet reassurance, and I knew that I had finally confronted the thing I had been running from for so long.

As the world faded to white, I felt a deep sense of peace settle over me.

I was finally free.

Chapter 29: Beneath the Surface

When the world of light faded away, I found myself standing in my living room again. Everything was as it had been before I stepped through the mirror: the quiet hum of the house, the soft flicker of the lamp casting gentle shadows on the walls. Yet, something had shifted inside me. There was a lightness I hadn't felt in years, as though the burdens I had carried for so long had finally been set down.

I had confronted my past—my real past, not just the shadows and fears of the mirror world. The reflection had guided me back to the things I had buried, things I had been too afraid to face. And now that I had, the grip of the mirror world seemed to loosen, as though it had served its purpose.

For the first time, I felt truly free.

But as the hours passed and the house grew still, I couldn't shake the feeling that something was still unresolved. The mirror, now just a piece of glass hanging on the wall, no longer held the same menace it once did. But it wasn't gone, either. I could feel its presence, faint but lingering, like a whisper at the back of my mind.

The reflection had told me that I had more to confront. I had faced my past, but the mirror world was still calling me. Something beneath the surface remained, something that I hadn't yet acknowledged.

I sat in the quiet of the evening, my mind turning over the events of the last few weeks. The mirror world had shown me my fears, my hidden memories, but it had also shown me a version of myself I had never known—calm, accepting, whole.

That version of me had been guiding me through the mirror world, helping me to face what I had hidden for so long. But now, with my past confronted, I was left wondering: what else was there?

As the night deepened, the sense of unease grew stronger. It wasn't fear, exactly, but a pull—an urge to go deeper, to uncover whatever lay hidden in the depths of the mirror world. I hadn't seen the reflection since I returned from the past, but its presence still lingered, just out of sight, waiting for me to take the next step.

I stood from the couch, feeling a sudden resolve settle over me. I knew what I had to do. The mirror world hadn't let me go completely, and I wasn't sure it ever would until I understood everything it had to show me.

I walked to the hallway, where the mirror hung in its usual place. The surface was still, reflecting only the dim light of the room. But I could feel the energy pulsing from it, faint but steady. I had come so far—further than I ever thought I could—but this last part, whatever it was, remained elusive.

I reached out and touched the glass, half-expecting the world to ripple beneath my hand. But the glass stayed solid, cold under my fingertips. I took a deep breath, closed my eyes, and pressed my palm against the mirror.

For a moment, nothing happened. The house was quiet, and the air felt still.

But then, slowly, I felt the shift.

The surface of the mirror grew warm beneath my hand, and the familiar pull of the mirror world began to tug at me. It wasn't as strong as before—not the overwhelming force that had dragged me in the first time—but it was there, beckoning me forward.

I opened my eyes, and the world around me shimmered, the edges of the room blurring and fading into darkness. The reflection in the mirror flickered, and for a moment, I thought I saw a figure standing just beyond the glass, watching me from the other side.

"Come," the whisper said, soft but unmistakable. "It's time."

I swallowed hard, my pulse quickening as I stepped closer to the mirror. I had thought I was done with the mirror world, thought I had confronted everything it had to show me. But something was waiting for me, something deeper, something hidden.

With a deep breath, I pressed my hand harder against the glass, and once again, I was pulled through.

The mirror world wasn't the same as it had been before. The chaotic, fractured landscape I had first encountered was gone, replaced by something more structured, more defined. I found myself standing in a long, narrow corridor, the walls lined with mirrors that stretched endlessly in both directions. Each mirror reflected the hallway back at me, creating an infinite loop of reflections that disappeared into the distance.

I walked forward slowly, my footsteps echoing softly against the cold, hard floor. The air here felt different—heavier, more charged, as though the space itself was alive with energy. As I moved deeper into the corridor, I noticed that the reflections in the mirrors weren't just of the hallway. They were reflections of **me**—but not the me I saw in the real world. Each reflection was different, showing a version of myself from a different time, a different moment in my life.

In one mirror, I saw myself as a child, wide-eyed and curious, standing in my childhood home. In another, I saw myself as a teenager, angry and confused, lost in the uncertainty of who I was becoming. And in yet another, I saw myself as I was now, older, more weathered, but also more aware.

I stopped in front of one of the mirrors, my heart pounding as I stared at the reflection. It showed me as I was in the present, but there was something different about this reflection. The eyes were darker, more intense, and the expression on my face wasn't one of peace—it was one of **sadness**. A deep, unresolved sadness that seemed to radiate from the reflection.

"What is this?" I whispered, my voice trembling.

The reflection didn't move, but the eyes seemed to lock onto mine, filled with a quiet intensity. I took a step closer, my breath catching in my throat. This wasn't just a reflection. This was something more—something I hadn't seen before.

And then, the reflection spoke.

"You've come so far," it said softly, the voice low and filled with emotion. "But there's still something you're not seeing."

I frowned, stepping closer to the mirror. "What do you mean?"

The reflection tilted its head slightly, the sadness in its eyes deepening. "You've confronted your past, but you haven't confronted your **future**."

I stared at the reflection, my mind racing. My future? I had spent so much time running from the things that had already happened, from the memories and the pain of my past. I had never even considered what lay ahead.

"I don't understand," I said, my voice barely a whisper. "What does my future have to do with the mirror world?"

The reflection smiled faintly, the expression filled with a quiet resignation. "The mirror world isn't just about the past. It's about everything—the past, the present, and the future. You've seen what you've been running from, but you haven't yet seen what you're running **toward**."

I took a deep breath, the weight of the words sinking in. I had always thought of the mirror world as a place that reflected the darkest parts of me—the things I had tried to forget, the fears I had buried. But now, standing here in front of this reflection, I realized that the mirror world wasn't just a reflection of the past. It was a reflection of **everything**—including the choices I hadn't yet made, the paths I hadn't yet walked.

The reflection stepped closer, its hand reaching out to touch the glass. "There's more to see," it said softly. "If you're ready."

I nodded slowly, my heart pounding in my chest. "I'm ready."

The reflection smiled, and the surface of the mirror shimmered, the glass rippling like water. I stepped forward, my hand reaching out to touch the reflection, and as I did, the world around me dissolved into light.

Chapter 30: The Weight of Tomorrow

The moment I touched the reflection, the light enveloped me once again, but this time it wasn't the blinding light of revelation. It was softer, gentler, as though it were cradling me, guiding me toward something I had yet to understand. The warmth of the light made the journey feel less like an intrusion and more like a transition—like I was stepping into something I had always known, but hadn't been ready to see.

When the light faded, I found myself standing in an entirely new place. The long, mirrored corridor was gone, replaced by a vast, open field stretching out in every direction. The sky above was a deep twilight blue, dotted with stars, and the air carried the cool scent of rain on the horizon. It was peaceful, quiet, yet there was something unmistakably charged about this place.

I looked down at my hands. I was still myself, whole and unbroken, but I felt lighter, as though the weight I had carried for so long had been lifted, if only for a moment. The reflection was gone. No guide, no echo of myself, just **me**—alone in this endless landscape of possibility.

I turned slowly, taking in the horizon, and that's when I saw it: **a path**, narrow but clear, winding its way through the field. It seemed to shimmer slightly, as though it weren't entirely fixed in place, as if the path itself were still deciding which way to turn. There was no clear end in sight, only the beginning, stretching out before me.

My heart pounded in my chest as I stepped toward the path. This was different from anything the mirror world had shown me before. There were no dark corners, no haunting reflections, no memories I had buried. This felt... new. Like the future itself had taken shape, waiting for me to step into it.

I took a deep breath and followed the path, my footsteps soft against the grass. The further I walked, the more I felt that pull again—not the violent pull of the mirror world trying to drag me into its depths, but a subtle, insistent tug at the edges of my mind. It wasn't forcing me forward, but it was guiding me, leading me toward something I couldn't yet see.

As I walked, the sky above shifted, the stars brightening, and the air around me grew cooler, sharper. The landscape, though beautiful, began to feel more uncertain. I realized that the path beneath my feet was no longer entirely steady. With each step, it seemed to shift slightly, as though the ground itself wasn't sure where I was headed.

And then, in the distance, I saw it: **a door**, standing alone in the middle of the field, its frame gleaming in the twilight. The door was slightly ajar, just as it had been the first time I encountered it in the mirror world. But this time, there was no ominous sense of danger, no looming threat. The door felt like a choice, not a trap.

I approached slowly, my heart pounding, my mind racing with possibilities. I knew, deep down, that this door wasn't just an exit or an entrance. It was a threshold—one I would have to cross if I wanted to understand what lay ahead.

When I reached the door, I paused, my hand hovering over the handle. For the first time since I entered the mirror world, I didn't feel the need to hesitate. I had come so far, faced so much, and now I knew that whatever lay beyond this door was the next step in understanding who I was and who I could become.

I pushed the door open, and the world beyond it shimmered into view.

The scene on the other side was one I didn't expect.

It was a version of my life, but not the life I had known. It was a future, a possible future, one that I hadn't imagined, but one that felt painfully real.

I stepped through the door and found myself standing in a small, familiar apartment. The room was filled with light, the kind of soft, golden light that made everything feel warm and safe. There was a sense of quiet calm in the air, as though this place were a sanctuary, untouched by the chaos of the world.

And then I saw **her**.

Sitting at the kitchen table, her back to me, was a woman. She was writing in a notebook, her hand moving slowly across the page. Her hair was dark, her posture relaxed, and though I couldn't see her face, I knew—**I knew**—who she was.

It was me.

But this wasn't just any version of myself. This was me, older, wiser, living a life that seemed far removed from the fears and doubts I had carried with me for so long. This was a future I hadn't allowed myself to imagine.

I took a step closer, my heart pounding in my chest. The older version of me didn't turn, didn't seem to notice my presence, but I felt her awareness. She knew I was there. She was waiting.

I stopped a few feet away from the table, my hands trembling. This version of me was calm, content. The lines on her face told a story of experience, of struggle, but also of peace. She had found something I had been searching for but hadn't yet reached. She had found a way to move forward.

I wanted to speak, to ask her how she had done it—how she had found her way out of the darkness. But the words wouldn't come. Instead, I simply stood there, watching her, feeling the weight of the moment settle over me.

After what felt like an eternity, she finally spoke, her voice soft but clear, like a distant echo of my own.

"You're afraid of what comes next," she said, not looking up from her notebook.

I swallowed hard, my throat tight. "I don't know what comes next."

She set the pen down and turned to face me. Her eyes were gentle, filled with the kind of understanding that only comes from having lived through the things I was still struggling with.

"No one does," she said. "But that's the point. You don't have to know everything to move forward. You just have to keep going."

I stared at her, the truth of her words sinking in. For so long, I had been paralyzed by fear—fear of the past, fear of the mirror world, fear of who I was becoming. But now, standing here, I realized that the fear had been a wall, something I had built to protect myself from the unknown. And in doing so, I had kept myself trapped.

"What if I can't do it?" I asked, my voice trembling.

She smiled—a small, knowing smile that felt both comforting and bittersweet. "You can. You will. But you have to let go of the idea that you need all the answers right now."

I felt a surge of emotion rise in my chest, a mixture of relief and sadness. This version of myself had walked the path I was only just beginning, and she had found peace on the other side. But the journey to that peace wasn't something I could rush. It was something I had to **live**.

"You'll make mistakes," she continued, her voice soft. "You'll doubt yourself. You'll fall. But you'll get up. And one day, you'll look back and realize that all the fear, all the uncertainty—it led you to where you needed to be."

I nodded slowly, tears burning in my eyes. "How do I start?"

She stood up from the table and walked over to me, her presence a quiet comfort. She placed a hand on my shoulder, her touch warm and reassuring.

"You've already started," she said. "Now, you just have to keep going."

I looked into her eyes and saw my future—not a perfect future, not one without challenges, but one where I had learned to live with myself, to accept the parts of me I had once feared. And in that future, I was okay.

I was **whole**.

I closed my eyes, the weight of her words settling over me like a blanket, and when I opened them again, the room was gone. The door, the apartment, the older version of myself—all of it had faded into the light.

I stood once again in the vast, open field, the path winding its way through the grass. The sky above was still twilight, still filled with stars, but now the air felt different—lighter, more open.

I took a deep breath and stepped forward, my feet finding the path once more. I didn't know where it would lead, and for the first time, that was okay.

I would keep going.

And I would be **ready**.

Chapter 31: A Door Left Open

The field, endless and quiet, stretched out before me as I stood once again on the path. The weight of the conversation with my future self lingered in my mind, a strange mixture of comfort and uncertainty settling deep in my chest. I had seen what I could become—calm, centered, at peace with my past and my future. Yet, the path I walked now felt as unpredictable as the wind, with every step leading into an unknown I couldn't fully grasp.

The stars above me were brighter now, their cold light casting long shadows over the grass. The air smelled of rain, fresh and clean, but heavy with a tension I couldn't name. I walked slowly, the soft crunch of grass beneath my feet the only sound breaking the stillness. I didn't know where I was headed, but I no longer felt the frantic urge to run, to escape. I was moving forward, and that was enough.

As I walked, I became aware of something ahead—a shadow on the horizon, barely visible at first but growing clearer with every step. I quickened my pace, curiosity tugging at me, though part of me still resisted, afraid of what might lie beyond.

When I finally reached it, I stopped, my breath catching in my throat.

It was **another door**.

Not the kind that led me into strange worlds or future visions, but a simple wooden door, worn and weathered by time. It stood alone in the field, its dark wood rough to the touch, with no frame or walls surrounding it. It was just... there, an impossible structure in an impossible place.

My heart pounded as I approached it, the memories of all the doors I had passed through in the mirror world swirling in my mind. Each one had led me deeper into a labyrinth of reflection, fear, and revelation. But this one felt different. There was no light spilling from beneath its frame, no ominous hum vibrating through the air. It was just a door, waiting for me to open it.

I reached for the handle, my fingers trembling as they brushed the cold metal. For a moment, I hesitated, unsure of what would happen if I crossed this threshold. Was it another part of the mirror world, or was this something new, something final?

I took a deep breath and pushed the door open.

The scene on the other side was nothing like the strange, dreamlike landscapes I had encountered before. It was **my life**, but not as I had left it. The apartment I had returned to after my journey into the mirror world was now different—filled with warmth, light, and a quiet sense of purpose that hadn't been there before. It felt like a place that was lived in, not just a temporary shelter.

I stepped through the door and into the apartment, my footsteps soft on the hardwood floor. The air was warm, carrying the faint smell of coffee and something sweet baking in the kitchen. Sunlight streamed through the windows, casting golden light across the floor, and the soft hum of everyday life filled the space.

It was familiar and foreign all at once.

I walked into the living room, my eyes scanning the walls, the furniture, the small details of this place. It was my apartment, but it wasn't. Everything was in its place, yet there were small differences—new books on the shelves, a stack of papers on the table, a photograph I didn't recognize. I moved closer to the photograph, picking it up gently.

It was a picture of **me**.

I was smiling, standing next to someone I didn't recognize—a man with kind eyes and a warm, open face. He was laughing, his arm around my shoulders, and in the picture, I looked... happy. Really happy. It was a version of myself I hadn't seen in a long time, maybe ever.

I set the photograph down carefully, my mind racing. Who was he? When had this happened? Was this a vision of another possible future, or was it something else entirely? I couldn't tell. Everything about this place felt so real, so immediate, as though I had just stepped into a version of my own life I hadn't yet lived.

I wandered through the apartment, my heart pounding in my chest, each step filled with a strange mixture of hope and fear. There were signs of life everywhere—clothes tossed casually over a chair, a cup of coffee half-drunk on the table, a stack of bills waiting to be paid. But it was more than that. The apartment felt **alive**, as though it had been filled with love and laughter, the kind of life I had never quite managed to build for myself before.

I moved into the kitchen, where the smell of something baking filled the air. A small pan of cookies sat cooling on the counter, steam rising from them in soft tendrils. I couldn't help but smile at the simple, domestic scene, but as I reached for one of the cookies, I froze.

Someone was standing in the doorway.

I turned slowly, my heart hammering in my chest.

It was the man from the photograph. He stood there, smiling softly, his eyes filled with warmth and understanding. He didn't seem surprised to see me, didn't ask how I had appeared in his life out of nowhere. Instead, he stepped forward, his hands outstretched as though he had been waiting for me all along.

"You're here," he said gently, his voice low and calm.

I blinked, confusion and emotion swelling inside me. "Where... where is here?"

He smiled, the kind of smile that seemed to carry years of knowing. "This is your life, or at least, it could be."

I shook my head, my thoughts spinning. "I don't understand."

He took a step closer, his presence soothing even as my mind raced. "You've been running for so long. You've been trapped in your past, in your fears, in the mirror world. But this—this is what happens when you stop running. When you choose to live."

I stared at him, tears burning in my eyes. "Is this real?"

He reached out and took my hand, his touch warm and grounding. "It's as real as you allow it to be."

I looked around the apartment, taking in every detail—the photographs, the small signs of a life shared, the quiet peace that filled the space. It felt so real, so close, but also so far away. Was this really what my life could become if I let go of the fear that had gripped me for so long? If I chose to live instead of hiding behind the mirrors?

"I don't know how," I whispered, my voice trembling. "I don't know how to get here."

He squeezed my hand gently, his eyes never leaving mine. "You do. You've already started. Every step you've taken, every fear you've faced—it's all led you to this moment. You just have to keep going."

I nodded slowly, the weight of his words sinking in. This place, this life—it wasn't out of reach. It was possible. But it wasn't something that could be given to me. It was something I had to choose, something I had to build, one step at a time.

I took a deep breath and let go of his hand, my heart feeling both heavier and lighter all at once. "Will I see you again?"

He smiled, a quiet sadness in his eyes. "You'll see me when you're ready. When you're truly ready to live this life."

I closed my eyes, the tears slipping down my cheeks as I nodded. When I opened them again, the apartment, the man, the warmth—all of it was fading, dissolving into light. The future I had seen was slipping away, but not in a way that felt like loss. It felt like possibility, like a door left open, waiting for me to walk through it when I was ready.

I stood in the field once again, the door behind me now closed but still there, waiting. The path stretched out before me, winding through the grass, and the sky above was darker now, the stars burning brighter in the twilight.

I wiped the tears from my face, my breath coming in slow, steady waves. I didn't know when I would find that life—the one I had seen on the other side of the door. But I knew now that it was possible, that it was something I could reach if I kept walking, kept choosing to move forward.

I took a deep breath and stepped onto the path once more.

The future was waiting.

And this time, I was ready.

Chapter 32: The Breaking of the Glass

When I stepped back onto the path, a weight I hadn't realized I was carrying seemed to lift from my shoulders. The door I had just passed through remained behind me, closed but not sealed, its presence a quiet reminder that the future I had glimpsed was still there, waiting for me when I was ready to fully embrace it.

The sky above had darkened further, the stars burning brighter against the deepening twilight. As I walked, the air around me felt more solid, more real, as though the world itself was slowly pulling me back from the dreamlike state of the mirror world. But there was something else—a shift in the energy around me, subtle but undeniable. The landscape, once soft and inviting, now seemed to pulse with a quiet tension, as though it was preparing for something.

I continued down the path, my steps slow and deliberate. The grass beneath my feet felt cool and damp, the scent of rain hanging in the air. I didn't know where I was going, but I knew that I had to keep moving. There was still something left to confront, something the mirror world hadn't yet shown me.

And then, in the distance, I saw it: **a figure**, standing still at the edge of the path.

My heart skipped a beat, a wave of recognition washing over me. The figure was tall, its outline blurred by the dim light, but I knew who it was. I had seen it before, in the mirrors, in the shadows. It was my **reflection**—the version of me that had guided me through the mirror world, helping me to face my fears, to confront the truths I had buried.

But this time, something was different.

As I approached, the figure didn't move, didn't speak. It stood there, watching me, its presence no longer comforting but filled with a strange, unsettling stillness. The reflection was waiting for me, just as it always had, but now there was a tension between us, an unspoken challenge hanging in the air.

When I was only a few feet away, I stopped, my breath catching in my throat. The reflection stood before me, its face obscured by the shadows, but I could feel its gaze locked on mine.

"You've come far," the reflection said, its voice calm but cold. "But you're not done yet."

I swallowed hard, my pulse quickening. "What do you mean?"

The reflection stepped forward, its movements slow and deliberate. "You've seen your past. You've glimpsed your future. But there's one last thing you haven't faced."

I frowned, confusion twisting in my gut. "What is it?"

The reflection tilted its head slightly, its expression unreadable. "Yourself."

I stared at the figure, my mind racing. I had spent so much time running from my reflection, fearing what it might show me. But now, after everything I had seen, after all the truths I had confronted, I didn't understand what was left.

"I've faced myself," I said, my voice shaking. "I've accepted who I am."

The reflection smiled—a small, cold smile that sent a shiver down my spine. "You've accepted what you've seen. But there's more to you than that."

THE SPACE BETWEEN THE MIRROR 165

Before I could respond, the reflection raised its hand, and the ground beneath my feet began to tremble. I stumbled back, my heart pounding in my chest, as the landscape around us started to shift and twist. The soft grass of the field gave way to jagged stone, the sky darkening to an inky blackness, and the air grew cold and sharp.

The path disappeared, and I found myself standing on the edge of a vast, broken landscape, the ground cracked and fractured, stretching out into a dark, endless horizon. The stars above were gone, replaced by swirling clouds of shadow and light, and the wind howled through the air, carrying with it the faintest echo of voices I couldn't understand.

I turned back to the reflection, panic rising in my chest. "What is this?"

"This," the reflection said, its voice low and dangerous, "is what you've been running from all along."

I took a step back, my mind spinning. "I don't understand. What are you talking about?"

The reflection stepped closer, its eyes burning with a strange, intense light. "You've spent so much time confronting the things that happened to you—the fears, the memories, the pain. But you've never truly faced the one thing that connects them all."

I shook my head, my breath coming in shallow gasps. "What is that?"

The reflection smiled again, the kind of smile that made my skin crawl. "Yourself."

I stared at the reflection, my pulse racing. "I don't understand. I've accepted who I am. I've faced my fears. What more is there?"

The reflection's eyes darkened, and the air around us seemed to grow heavier, thicker. "You've faced the parts of yourself that you were willing to see. But you haven't faced the truth of who you really are."

I felt a cold shiver run down my spine. "And what is that?"

The reflection stepped even closer, until it was only inches away from me. Its presence was overwhelming, suffocating, and I could feel the weight of its gaze pressing down on me, filling the space between us with a tension I couldn't escape.

"You are the one who broke yourself," the reflection whispered. "You are the one who shattered everything."

I stumbled back, my heart pounding in my chest, my mind reeling from the weight of the words. "That's not true," I whispered, shaking my head. "I didn't—"

"You did," the reflection said, its voice cutting through the air like a knife. "You've been running from the truth for so long, blaming the mirror world, blaming your past. But the truth is, you broke yourself. You shattered your own reflection."

I felt the ground tremble beneath me, the cracks in the earth widening, the shadows closing in. "No," I whispered, tears burning in my eyes. "I didn't mean to. I didn't—"

"You did," the reflection repeated, its voice cold and relentless. "You shattered your own soul. You broke the pieces of yourself that you couldn't bear to face. And now, you're left with nothing but fragments."

I collapsed to my knees, the weight of the truth crashing down on me like a tidal wave. The mirror world, the fear, the memories—it had all been leading to this moment. The reflection wasn't just a part of me. It was me. And I had been the one to break myself, to fracture my own identity, to hide the pieces I didn't want to see.

"I'm sorry," I whispered, my voice trembling. "I didn't know."

The reflection knelt beside me, its presence no longer cold, but filled with a strange, quiet sadness. "You've been running for so long," it said softly. "But you don't have to run anymore. You can put the pieces back together."

I looked up at the reflection, my vision blurred by tears. "How?"

The reflection reached out, placing a hand gently on my shoulder. "By accepting the brokenness. By embracing the parts of yourself that you've been trying to hide. You don't have to be whole. You just have to be **you**."

I closed my eyes, the tears slipping down my cheeks as the words sank in. For so long, I had been trying to fix myself, to heal the wounds I had carried, to become whole again. But now, standing on the edge of this broken world, I realized that I didn't need to be perfect. I just needed to be **me**, broken pieces and all.

I opened my eyes and looked at the reflection, the sadness in its eyes mirroring my own. "I'm ready," I said, my voice steady despite the tears. "I'm ready to put the pieces back together."

The reflection smiled, a small, genuine smile that filled me with a quiet sense of peace. "Then let's begin."

The ground beneath us trembled one last time, and the cracks in the earth began to close. The swirling shadows in the sky faded, replaced by the soft, familiar light of the stars. The landscape shifted again, the jagged stone giving way to smooth, gentle grass, and the cold wind was replaced by a warm, comforting breeze.

I stood, my legs unsteady but strong, and faced the reflection.

It was time to let go of the broken pieces.

And it was time to become **whole**—not in the way I had once imagined, but in the way that only I could define.

Together, we walked forward.

Chapter 33: The Path of Wholeness

As I walked alongside my reflection, a profound sense of calm settled over me. The landscape around us transformed into a serene expanse of soft grass underfoot, the night sky overhead now filled with bright, twinkling stars that sparkled like distant promises. The air was warm, and a gentle breeze brushed against my skin, carrying with it the faint scent of blooming flowers. It felt like stepping into a dream, one where everything was finally in its right place.

We moved together, my reflection and I, side by side, no longer separated by the barrier of glass or the weight of fear. I could feel the connection between us growing stronger with each step, as though the line that had once divided my past, present, and future was beginning to blur into one cohesive journey.

"Where are we going?" I asked, my voice steady, filled with a sense of newfound purpose.

"To a place where you can truly begin to heal," my reflection replied, its voice a gentle echo of my own. "A place where you can accept all the parts of yourself—those you've hidden and those you've embraced."

I nodded, the anticipation bubbling within me. It was time to face not just my fears but also the hope that lay dormant within me. We walked on, and with every step, I could feel the fragments of my past slowly coming together, forming a clearer picture of who I was meant to be.

As we moved through the field, I began to notice changes in the landscape. The gentle grass gave way to a winding path lined with trees, their branches heavy with blossoms that swayed in the breeze. The air filled with the sweet fragrance of flowers, and the sound of laughter floated through the air like a melody, inviting me to come closer.

"What is this place?" I asked, my heart racing with excitement.

"This is a reflection of your heart," the figure said. "A place where the joys and sorrows of your past can coexist, where you can learn to embrace everything that has shaped you."

We continued down the path, the laughter growing louder, and soon we arrived at a clearing. It was filled with people—friends, family, faces from my past and present—each one vibrant and alive. They moved with a joyful energy, their laughter infectious as they danced and celebrated under the moonlight.

I felt a rush of emotion as I recognized them. Memories flooded back—moments of love, laughter, and connection. People I had cherished but had also distanced myself from in my struggle to cope with my fears and insecurities.

"Join them," my reflection urged, stepping aside as I stood on the edge of the clearing, heart pounding in my chest. "This is part of you, too."

I hesitated for a moment, uncertainty creeping in. But the warmth of their joy was overwhelming, and I felt a pull toward them—a magnetic connection that reminded me of the beauty of human experience. I stepped forward into the clearing, the laughter enveloping me like a warm embrace.

As I entered the circle of light, the music swelled, and the people turned to me, their smiles wide and welcoming. I felt tears prick at the corners of my eyes as I recognized each face, each moment shared.

"Welcome home," one voice said, a gentle reminder that I was never truly lost.

The realization washed over me like a wave. I had spent so long running from my past, from the pain and the memories that had haunted me. But here, surrounded by the people who had shaped my life, I felt a sense of belonging that had eluded me for so long. I was not alone.

I joined the dance, laughter bubbling up from deep within me as I twirled and spun, the joy of being alive coursing through my veins. I let go of the burdens I had carried for too long, allowing the music to lift me higher, to carry me into a realm where pain and joy could coexist.

In that moment, I understood the beauty of wholeness. It was not about erasing the past or pretending it didn't exist; it was about embracing every part of myself, the light and the dark, the joy and the sorrow. It was about accepting that I was not just a reflection of my fears but a tapestry woven from every experience, every connection, every laugh, and every tear.

As the music swelled, I felt a presence beside me. I turned to see my reflection dancing with me, its smile filled with warmth and understanding. We were no longer separate; we were one, united in the journey of becoming.

The dance continued, and as I moved with the rhythm of the music, I began to see visions of the future flashing before me—small moments of everyday life, the laughter of friends, the warmth of family, the beauty of connection. Each vision was a reminder that life was a series of moments, each one precious and unique.

But then, amid the joy, a flicker of darkness passed through my mind—a reminder of the mirror world, the shadows that still lurked on the edges of my consciousness. I felt a momentary flash of fear, the remnants of the struggle that had brought me here.

But as I looked around at the faces of those I loved, I felt the fear begin to dissolve. The laughter, the joy, the love—they were stronger than the shadows. They anchored me, reminding me that I had the power to face whatever lay ahead.

I took a deep breath, grounding myself in the present moment, and let the warmth of the clearing wash over me. The darkness had taught me valuable lessons, but it didn't have to define me. I was ready to move forward, to embrace every piece of who I was—broken, beautiful, and whole.

And as I danced under the stars, surrounded by the people I loved, I knew that the path ahead, while uncertain, was filled with possibility. I was ready to face the challenges that lay ahead, to step into my future with courage and grace.

Together with my reflection, I twirled and spun, celebrating not just the journey I had taken, but the journey that was yet to come.

Chapter 34: The Final Pieces

As the music faded and the celebration in the clearing softened to a gentle hum, I found myself standing at the edge of the dance, watching as the people I loved continued to laugh and move with the rhythm of the night. My heart swelled with a warmth I hadn't felt in years—a kind of wholeness that extended beyond just myself. This was the feeling of connection, of being part of something larger than my own fears.

But even as I stood there, a subtle unease tugged at the edges of my mind. The joy of the moment, the beauty of the reunion—it was all real, all deeply felt. Yet, I couldn't shake the sensation that something remained unresolved. There was a lingering presence, a faint pull from the shadows, reminding me that I still had one last truth to face.

I took a deep breath and turned away from the clearing. My reflection, who had been dancing beside me, now stood silently at my side, watching me with quiet understanding. We didn't need to speak. It was clear that the celebration was not the final step. There was more.

With a gentle nod from my reflection, I walked toward the edge of the clearing, the laughter and music growing fainter behind me as I moved into the quiet, still night. The path before me stretched out like a ribbon of uncertainty, winding through the darkness, lit only by the faint glow of the stars above.

The deeper I walked into the night, the more the sense of unease grew. The landscape around me was changing again, no longer the peaceful, welcoming field I had come to know. The trees loomed larger, their branches reaching out like skeletal fingers, casting long shadows across the ground. The air grew colder, and the soft rustling of leaves was replaced by the distant echo of something far more ominous.

I continued forward, my steps slow but deliberate, the pull of the mirror world growing stronger with each passing moment. I knew that this path was leading me back to the darkness, to the place where I had first confronted my fears. But this time, I was not afraid.

I had faced the broken pieces of myself. I had embraced my past and glimpsed my future. But there was one final truth that the mirror world had yet to show me—one final piece of the puzzle that I hadn't yet put together.

As I walked, the landscape around me grew more distorted, the shadows twisting and bending in ways that defied logic. The air was thick with tension, as though the world itself was holding its breath, waiting for me to reach the end of the path. And then, in the distance, I saw it: **a mirror**, standing alone in the middle of the darkened landscape.

My heart pounded in my chest as I approached the mirror. It was tall, its surface smooth and pristine, reflecting nothing but the darkness around it. There was no frame, no ornate design—just a simple, unadorned mirror, waiting for me.

I stopped in front of it, my breath shallow as I stared at my reflection. But what I saw wasn't just **me**. It was every version of me that I had encountered along the way. The frightened child, the angry teenager, the broken adult, the serene guide, the future self—all of them were there, layered one over the other, creating a mosaic of faces, emotions, and experiences.

It was overwhelming. To see all of these versions of myself at once, to witness the full spectrum of my life reflected back at me in such stark detail—it felt like standing at the edge of an abyss. But instead of recoiling, I leaned in, my fingers brushing the cold surface of the glass.

And as I touched the mirror, the reflection shifted. The layers of faces and memories dissolved, leaving behind only one reflection: **me**, as I was now. No distortions, no shadows—just me, standing there, whole and unbroken.

I felt a wave of emotion rise within me—relief, sadness, hope—all swirling together in a perfect storm of realization. This was the final truth. This was what the mirror world had been trying to show me all along.

"I see it now," I whispered, my voice trembling with the weight of the moment. "I see myself."

The mirror shimmered in response, and for the first time, I understood. The mirror world had never been about trapping me, about pulling me into its depths. It had been about showing me what I had refused to see—the pieces of myself that I had hidden away, the truths I had buried beneath layers of fear and doubt.

I had been broken, yes. But I had also been whole. Every version of me, every face I had encountered along the way—they were all part of who I was. And now, standing here in front of the mirror, I realized that I didn't need to be afraid of those pieces anymore.

I was all of them, and I was none of them. I was more than the sum of my parts.

I took a deep breath and stepped back from the mirror, the tension in the air slowly dissipating. The shadows around me began to fade, and the coldness that had clung to the night lifted, replaced by a gentle warmth that spread through my entire body.

My reflection remained in the mirror, watching me with calm, steady eyes. There was no malice, no threat—just a quiet understanding. This was the reflection I had feared for so long, the one that had haunted me in the darkest moments of my life. But now, as I looked into its eyes, I realized that it was simply a part of me—a part that I no longer needed to run from.

"You've found your way," the reflection said softly, its voice a gentle echo of my own.

I nodded, tears slipping down my cheeks. "Yes," I whispered. "I have."

The reflection smiled, a small, knowing smile that filled me with a sense of peace I hadn't known was possible. "It's time."

With those words, the mirror began to shimmer, its surface rippling like water. I watched as the reflection slowly dissolved, the glass growing brighter and brighter until it was filled with a soft, golden light.

I stepped forward, the warmth of the light enveloping me as I reached out to touch the mirror one last time. And as my fingers brushed the glass, the world around me shifted, the darkness melting away into the brightness of a new dawn.

When I opened my eyes, I was back in my apartment.

The quiet hum of the world greeted me, the soft light of morning filtering through the curtains. I stood in the middle of the living room, the familiar weight of reality settling over me like a blanket.

But something was different.

I no longer felt the pull of the mirror world. The fear, the doubt, the endless cycle of running from myself—it was gone. In its place was a sense of calm, a sense of **wholeness** that I had never known before.

I walked over to the mirror on the wall, the same mirror that had once been the gateway to the world that had haunted me for so long. But now, as I stood in front of it, I saw only **me**—no distortions, no shadows, just my reflection staring back at me, whole and complete.

For the first time in a long time, I smiled—a real, genuine smile.

I had faced the darkness, the broken pieces of myself, and I had come out the other side.

I was ready to live again.

Chapter 35: The Quiet Echo

The morning light streamed softly through the windows, casting a golden hue over the apartment. For the first time in what felt like an eternity, I stood in front of the mirror without a trace of fear. It reflected me back exactly as I was: whole, steady, calm. My heart no longer raced at the sight of my own face, and the lingering shadows that once haunted the edges of my mind had lifted.

But as I stood there, a quiet echo reverberated within me. Though I had faced the darkest parts of myself, though I had seen the mirror world for what it was—a guide, not a threat—something remained unsettled. It wasn't fear or doubt this time. It was more like the faint whisper of unfinished business, a small voice reminding me that the journey wasn't quite over.

I turned away from the mirror and walked toward the living room. The apartment was bathed in the warm light of early morning, the remnants of my old life mingling with the new sense of clarity I had found. The weight that had once pressed down on my chest had lifted, but the echo remained. It was gentle but insistent, a quiet pull urging me to go deeper, to find the source of the lingering question I had yet to answer.

I settled into the couch, staring out the window at the city waking up around me. The world outside looked unchanged, the same buildings, the same streets, but I was different. And yet, as much as I wanted to believe that the mirror world had given me all the answers I needed, I couldn't shake the feeling that one final piece was still missing.

And then, in the silence of the apartment, I heard it.

A **knock**.

It was soft, almost hesitant, as if whoever stood on the other side wasn't sure they should be there. My heart skipped a beat, and I stood slowly, the echo growing louder in my chest. The knock came again, a little firmer this time, and I felt that familiar pull—the same pull that had drawn me into the mirror world in the first place.

I walked to the door, each step deliberate, as though I were crossing some invisible threshold between the world I had just left behind and the one waiting for me. My hand hovered over the doorknob for a moment, my breath catching in my throat. Whatever was on the other side of the door, I knew it would change everything. The mirror world had shown me the truth, but this—this was something else entirely.

With a deep breath, I turned the handle and opened the door.

Standing there, on the threshold of my apartment, was **her**. My reflection.

But it wasn't the version of myself I had faced in the mirror world. This was the real me—flesh and blood, solid and present, just as I was. She stood there, her eyes wide with uncertainty, her hands clasped tightly together in front of her. It was as though she had stepped out of the mirror and crossed into my world, leaving behind the ethereal quality of the reflection for something far more tangible.

I stared at her, my mind racing to make sense of what I was seeing. She looked exactly like me, down to the smallest detail, but there was a softness to her that I hadn't expected, a vulnerability in her eyes that mirrored the vulnerability I had felt in the mirror world.

"Hello," she said, her voice soft but clear.

I blinked, unable to find the words. "Who... who are you?"

She smiled faintly, her gaze steady but filled with something like understanding. "I'm you," she said simply. "But I'm also something more."

I stepped back, my heart pounding in my chest. "I don't understand. I thought... I thought I had accepted all of this. I thought the mirror world was over."

Her smile widened, but there was a sadness in it, too. "The mirror world was never about the ending. It was about the beginning. You've accepted yourself, yes, but you've only just scratched the surface. There's still more."

I shook my head, trying to piece together the fragments of what she was saying. "What more could there be? I faced my fears. I've seen who I am. I'm ready to move on."

She stepped inside, closing the door softly behind her, and for a moment, we stood there in silence, two versions of the same person in the same room. I felt a strange sense of calm wash over me, even as the questions buzzed in my mind.

"You've seen the pieces of yourself that you were willing to face," she said, her voice gentle. "But there's one part of you that you've been avoiding."

I frowned, the weight of her words settling over me like a heavy blanket. "What part?"

She stepped closer, her gaze unwavering. "The part that doesn't want to be whole."

I recoiled, the truth of her words hitting me like a punch to the gut. "What do you mean?"

Her eyes softened, and she reached out, taking my hand in hers. Her touch was warm, grounding, and I felt the connection between us deepen.

"You've spent so long trying to put the pieces back together," she said quietly. "But what if the pieces were never meant to fit perfectly? What if you're meant to embrace the cracks, the flaws, the parts of you that will never be fully healed?"

I stared at her, my heart aching with the weight of her words. "But I thought... I thought the whole point was to become whole again. To fix what's broken."

She smiled, and this time, it was a smile filled with warmth and understanding. "No one is ever truly whole. And that's okay. You don't have to be fixed. You just have to **be**. To live, to experience, to embrace the messiness of it all."

I felt tears welling up in my eyes as the truth of what she was saying sank in. For so long, I had been chasing the idea of wholeness, of perfection. I had believed that if I could just piece myself back together, I would finally be okay. But now, standing here in front of this version of myself, I realized that wholeness wasn't the goal.

The goal was to **live**.

"I'm not broken," I whispered, the tears spilling down my cheeks.

She nodded, her own eyes glistening with unshed tears. "No, you're not. You're just human."

We stood there for a long moment, the silence between us filled with an unspoken understanding. And in that moment, I realized that the journey I had been on wasn't about fixing myself. It was about learning to live with the cracks, the imperfections, the parts of me that would always be unfinished.

I wiped the tears from my face and smiled, a real, genuine smile that came from deep within me. "Thank you," I whispered, my voice filled with gratitude.

She smiled back, the warmth in her eyes reflecting my own. "You don't need to thank me. You've had the answers all along."

I nodded, feeling a deep sense of peace settle over me. For the first time in a long time, I felt like I was exactly where I was meant to be.

And as I stood there, holding hands with the reflection of myself, I knew that the journey wasn't over. It would never be over. But that was okay. Because I was no longer running from the pieces of myself that didn't fit perfectly. I was embracing them.

I was **living**.

Chapter 36: The Crack in the Glass

The quiet of the apartment settled around me like a comforting blanket as I sat in the dim morning light, the reflection of myself—the real, flesh-and-blood version—seated across from me. The conversation we had shared still echoed in my mind, each word, each truth unraveling the final layers of my long-held beliefs. The idea that I didn't need to be perfectly whole or fixed had lodged itself deep in my heart, but that didn't mean I understood it fully.

I had spent so long chasing wholeness, believing it was something I could achieve through confrontation, through healing, through fixing the broken parts of myself. But now, the reflection's words echoed back at me: **You don't have to be fixed. You just have to be.**

The reflection stood up from the chair and walked to the window, her hand resting on the frame as she looked out into the world. I watched her for a long moment, trying to understand what came next. I had faced the darkness of the mirror world. I had embraced the broken pieces of myself. But now, standing on the other side of that journey, I found myself wondering how to live in this new understanding.

"What happens now?" I asked quietly, my voice barely above a whisper.

The reflection didn't turn to look at me, but her voice was soft when she replied. "Now, you live. You go out into the world and live with everything you've learned. You stop searching for the perfect version of yourself and start accepting the one who's here right now."

I nodded slowly, the truth of her words sinking in. The journey I had taken into the mirror world had been about facing the darkness and the fear that had haunted me for so long. But the real challenge—the real test—wasn't just confronting the shadows. It was learning how to exist in the light afterward.

I stood and joined her by the window, the morning sun casting long beams of light through the glass. The city outside was coming to life—people walking on the sidewalks, cars rushing by, the hum of normal life carrying on without pause. I had been inside this cocoon of self-discovery for so long that the idea of stepping back into the world felt almost foreign.

"Living isn't as easy as it sounds," I said quietly.

The reflection turned to me, her eyes soft but unwavering. "No, it's not. It's messy and complicated. But that's what makes it real."

I stared out at the city, a soft sigh escaping my lips. "What if I don't know how? What if I slip back into the old patterns, the old fears?"

She smiled, and this time there was no sadness in it—only warmth. "You will slip sometimes. You'll fall. You'll question everything all over again. But now, you know how to get back up. You know that it's okay to be imperfect."

I looked into her eyes, seeing the reflection of all the versions of myself I had met along the way—the frightened child, the angry teenager, the woman who had been lost in fear and doubt. They were all there, but none of them defined me completely. They were parts of me, yes, but they weren't the whole story.

"I guess I've been afraid of failing," I admitted.

The reflection nodded, her gaze filled with understanding. "Everyone is. But failure isn't the end. It's part of the process."

I leaned against the window frame, the glass cool against my skin. "You make it sound so simple."

She laughed softly. "It's not simple. But it's worth it."

We stood there in silence for a long moment, watching the world outside move forward in its quiet, predictable way. I had been so focused on the internal battles, on the journey within, that I had forgotten what it felt like to be part of the world around me. The mirror world had taken me deep into myself, but now it was time to return to something bigger than just my own fears and struggles.

I glanced at her, a thought tugging at the edge of my mind. "Will I see you again? After this?"

Her expression softened. "You'll always see me. Maybe not like this, not in the form of a reflection, but I'm always with you. I am you."

I nodded, the weight of her words settling over me like a final piece of the puzzle. She wasn't just a reflection in the mirror anymore. She was a part of me, a part I had learned to accept, a part that would always be there even if I couldn't always see her.

As we stood there, the light streaming through the window, I noticed something strange. A small, almost imperceptible **crack** ran down the length of the glass. It hadn't been there before, and it was barely visible, but now that I had noticed it, I couldn't look away.

I reached out and touched the crack, my fingers tracing the delicate line. It wasn't broken, not completely. It was just a tiny flaw in an otherwise perfect window, a reminder that even the clearest glass can have its imperfections.

The reflection watched me, her expression thoughtful. "The crack isn't something to fix," she said softly. "It's part of the story now."

I looked at her, understanding dawning slowly. The crack in the glass was a symbol, a reminder that even when we seem whole, there will always be small imperfections. But those imperfections didn't need to be mended or hidden. They were part of the journey. They were part of being human.

"I'm not afraid of it anymore," I said, my voice steady.

She smiled. "That's because you've learned that it's okay to be imperfect."

I nodded, my heart lighter than it had been in years. The crack in the glass wasn't something to fear. It was a reminder that I had survived, that I had faced the darkness and come out the other side. I was still standing, still whole, even with all my flaws.

We stood there together, the reflection and I, watching the world outside the window. The crack in the glass caught the light, casting a faint shadow across the room, but it didn't detract from the beauty of the morning. It was simply **there**, a quiet testament to everything I had been through, everything I had learned.

"I think I'm ready," I said softly.

The reflection nodded, her smile gentle. "Then it's time to live."

I took a deep breath and turned away from the window, feeling the weight of the past lift from my shoulders as I stepped into the light of the new day. The reflection stayed behind, watching me with a quiet smile, but I knew she would always be with me, even when I couldn't see her.

I walked through the apartment, the familiar sounds and smells of home grounding me in the present. The mirror on the wall caught my eye as I passed, but I didn't stop to look into it. I didn't need to. I knew who I was now, flaws and all.

As I opened the door and stepped outside, the sunlight warmed my face, and I smiled.

The journey wasn't over. It would never truly be over. But now, I wasn't afraid of the cracks, the imperfections, the moments of doubt. I was ready to live—not in search of perfection, but in acceptance of everything that made me who I was.

And that, I realized, was more than enough.

Chapter 37: The Space Between

The world outside the apartment was bathed in sunlight, the kind that fills the air with a quiet sense of possibility. As I stepped out onto the street, the sounds of life greeted me—the hum of cars, the distant chatter of people walking to work, the rhythmic tap of footsteps on pavement. It felt different today. Not because the world had changed, but because **I** had.

For the first time in a long time, I walked without the weight of fear pressing down on my shoulders. There was no mirror world lurking in the corners of my vision, no shadows waiting to pull me back into the depths of my own mind. The world was just the world. And I was here, fully present, breathing in the crisp morning air and feeling the warmth of the sun on my skin.

As I moved through the streets, I felt a strange kind of freedom, like a bird that had been caged for too long and was finally able to stretch its wings. I had spent so much time trapped in my own reflections, in the endless cycle of trying to fix myself, that I had forgotten what it felt like to **live**. But now, as I walked through the city, I felt the first stirrings of life returning to me.

I passed by familiar places—shops, cafes, parks—each one filled with memories. Some were good, some were tinged with sadness, but none of them held the power over me that they once did. I wasn't running anymore. I wasn't hiding from the parts of myself that hurt. I wasn't avoiding the cracks.

Instead, I was learning to live in the **space between**—between the past and the future, between the moments of joy and sorrow, between the flaws and the strengths that made me who I was.

It wasn't easy. As I moved through the world, I could feel the familiar pull of doubt, the small voices in the back of my mind that whispered questions. **What if you fall again? What if the shadows come back?** But this time, those questions didn't shake me. They were part of the process. Part of being human.

As I reached the park, I found a quiet bench near the fountain and sat down, watching as the world moved around me. People walked by, their lives unfolding in ways I couldn't understand but felt connected to. There was something comforting in the knowledge that everyone was navigating their own path, their own mirror worlds, even if they didn't realize it. We were all just people, trying to find our way in a world that didn't always make sense.

I closed my eyes for a moment, letting the sounds of the city wash over me. The wind rustled through the trees, carrying with it the scent of freshly cut grass and blooming flowers. It was peaceful. Not in a grand, transformative way, but in a quiet, subtle way that reminded me that peace didn't have to be perfect. It could be found in the smallest of moments, in the space between everything else.

After a while, I opened my eyes and watched as a child ran across the park, laughing as they chased after a butterfly. Their laughter was pure, unburdened by the weight of the world, and it brought a smile to my face. I had forgotten how simple joy could be—how easy it was to find happiness in the little things.

As I sat there, watching life unfold around me, I realized that this was the heart of everything I had been searching for.

Not perfection. Not a life without cracks. But a life lived fully, in all its messiness and beauty.

I leaned back on the bench, feeling the warmth of the sun on my face, and allowed myself to breathe deeply, to feel the world around me and the world within me. There was still work to be done, still questions to answer, but for the first time in a long time, I wasn't rushing to find the answers. I was content to let them come in their own time.

The reflection had been right. Life wasn't about fixing everything or becoming perfectly whole. It was about living in the spaces between, accepting that I didn't need to have everything figured out, and finding peace in the journey itself.

After what felt like hours, I stood from the bench and continued walking. The day stretched out before me, filled with the potential of the unknown. And as I moved through the city, I felt a quiet excitement building within me. Not because everything was resolved, but because I was ready to face whatever came next.

As I walked, I noticed the reflection of myself in a storefront window. It wasn't the twisted, haunting reflection I had once feared. It was just **me**, looking back with a calm, steady gaze. For a moment, I paused, meeting my own eyes in the glass. There was no longer any tension, no longer any sense of being trapped. Just a quiet understanding that I was here, that I had faced my fears, and that I was ready to move forward.

I smiled at the reflection, not out of relief or triumph, but out of acceptance. I wasn't perfect, and I never would be. But I was learning to live with that, to embrace the cracks and the flaws, to find peace in the space between.

As I turned away from the window, I caught a glimpse of something in the corner of my vision—a flash of light, like the glint of sun on glass. I stopped, turning to look more closely, but whatever it was had already disappeared. I stood there for a moment, my heart beating a little faster, wondering if the mirror world had left behind one final trace.

But as I stood there, waiting, I realized that it didn't matter. Whether the mirror world was truly gone or whether it would always be part of me, I was ready. Ready to live, to face whatever came next, to embrace the uncertainty.

The space between the past and the future was where I lived now. And it was enough.

Chapter 38: Echoes of the Mirror

The day stretched into the afternoon, and as I continued walking through the city, I felt something different—something subtle but undeniable. It wasn't the kind of shift that shook the ground beneath me or pulled me back into the dark folds of the mirror world. It was quieter than that. It was as though the world had taken on a new texture, a softness I hadn't noticed before, a gentleness in the way light filtered through the trees, in the way the city moved around me.

The mirror world, with all its tangled reflections and fractured pieces, felt distant now, like an old dream I could still remember but no longer feared. And yet, even in its distance, there was a sense that it was still with me—an echo, a soft reminder that it had always been a part of my journey, even if it no longer held me in its grasp.

I turned down a quiet side street, away from the noise and bustle of the main road. Here, the world seemed to slow down. The street was lined with small, old shops and cafés, their windows reflecting the sun in a way that felt comforting, not foreboding. The reflections no longer unnerved me. I glanced at them as I passed, but each time, it was just **me**—the real me—looking back.

I stopped in front of a small café with large windows, the kind that invited you in with the smell of freshly brewed coffee and warm pastries. The sign above the door was simple: **Reflections Café**. I smiled at the name, feeling the irony settle over me like a gentle embrace. Maybe, in another life, I would

THE SPACE BETWEEN THE MIRROR 193

have avoided a place like this—a name like that. But now, it seemed like a fitting place to pause, to take a breath.

I pushed open the door and stepped inside. The warmth of the café wrapped around me immediately, the soft murmur of voices and the clink of cups creating a gentle, welcoming atmosphere. I ordered a cup of coffee and found a seat by the window, where the light poured in and made everything feel golden and calm.

As I sat there, sipping my coffee, I found myself watching the world outside. People moved in and out of view, their lives continuing as they always had. Some hurried past, lost in their own thoughts, while others paused to chat or simply enjoy the day. I felt a strange connection to them all—not because I knew them, but because I understood now that we were all navigating our own mirrors, our own internal landscapes.

The mirror world had been my crucible, my place of transformation, but I realized now that it wasn't unique to me. Everyone had their own version of it, whether they saw it or not. The challenges, the fears, the doubts—they were universal. We all faced them in different ways. And for the first time, I didn't feel alone in that understanding.

As I sat there, lost in thought, I felt a presence at the edge of my awareness. I didn't jump or panic. Instead, I looked up slowly, my eyes drawn to the reflection in the window across from me.

At first, it seemed like nothing more than my own reflection, but then, out of the corner of my eye, I saw **her**. My reflection—the one who had guided me through the mirror world, the one who had helped me piece myself back together—stood just behind me, her image faint but unmistakable in the glass.

She wasn't haunting me. She wasn't looming or threatening. She simply stood there, watching me with the same calm, understanding expression she had always worn. A reminder, not an intrusion.

I turned slightly in my seat, looking directly into the window's reflection, and for a moment, we just stared at each other. It was strange, but also comforting. She was a part of me, after all—always had been, always would be.

"I thought you might come back," I said softly, my voice barely above a whisper, knowing she could hear me even if she wasn't truly there.

Her smile was small, barely a curve of her lips, but it was filled with warmth. "I never really left," she replied, her voice echoing in my mind as much as in the glass.

I nodded, a soft laugh escaping me. "I guess not."

She didn't speak again, and I didn't feel the need to fill the silence. Instead, we just sat there together, my reflection and I, watching the world move outside the window. There was no tension between us now, no fear or resistance. Just quiet acceptance. I didn't need her to leave, and she didn't need to pull me back into the mirror world. We had found our balance.

I finished my coffee and stood to leave, pausing for one last moment at the window. My reflection remained, a gentle presence watching over me, but as I stepped away, she slowly faded from view, blending into the light until she was gone.

I left the café and continued down the street, feeling lighter with every step. The mirror world, once a place of fear and uncertainty, had become a memory—a part of me, but no longer something that controlled me. It was just a piece of the larger picture, a chapter in the story of who I was.

As I walked, the city opened up before me, the streets and buildings stretching out like endless possibilities. I didn't know where I was going, but for the first time, I didn't need to. The path wasn't about the destination anymore. It was about the journey, the spaces in between, the quiet moments of reflection that reminded me to keep moving forward.

I paused at a crosswalk, watching the light change from red to green. The people around me moved with purpose, each one following their own path, their own story. And I was just one of them—another person moving through life, navigating the echoes of my own reflections.

As I crossed the street, I caught one last glimpse of a reflection in the glass of a nearby building. It wasn't my reflection, but it reminded me of her—the faint echo of the person I had been and the person I was still becoming.

I smiled to myself and kept walking, the sun warm on my face, the world open before me.

Chapter 39: The Last Reflection

The afternoon sun had begun its slow descent, casting long shadows across the city as I continued my walk. The streets had quieted, the usual hustle and bustle giving way to the calm rhythm of a city winding down for the evening. I moved through it all with a quiet confidence, my steps light, my mind clear. There was no rush anymore, no pressing need to find answers. I was learning to live in the moment, to let each step unfold as it would.

The reflection from the café lingered in my thoughts—not as something ominous, but as a quiet reminder of where I had been, who I had become, and the journey I had taken. The mirror world was part of me now, woven into the fabric of my story, but it no longer controlled me. It no longer held the power it once did. I was free, not from the echoes of the past, but from the need to fight them.

As I approached a familiar corner, a street I had walked down many times before, I felt a faint pull, like a gentle tug at the edges of my consciousness. I stopped and looked around, my eyes landing on a small alleyway off to the side. It was narrow and dark, flanked by brick walls that seemed older than the buildings around them. There was nothing particularly special about it—just an ordinary alley in the middle of an ordinary city.

But something about it felt different today.

I hesitated for a moment, my heart skipping a beat, and then I stepped toward the alley. The closer I got, the more the pull intensified, a quiet whisper in the back of my mind urging me forward. It wasn't fear that drove me now—it was curiosity. A part of me knew that this alley, this unremarkable space, held something important.

As I stepped into the shadows, the noise of the city faded, replaced by a soft, almost imperceptible hum. The air grew cooler, and the light from the setting sun barely reached the walls around me. It felt like stepping into a forgotten place, a place that had been waiting for me all along.

At the end of the alley, nestled between two weathered brick buildings, was a small, round mirror.

It was unassuming, its frame made of tarnished silver, the kind of mirror you might find in an antique shop. It hung on the wall, catching the faintest glimmers of light from the street behind me, its surface reflecting the alley in perfect clarity.

I took a deep breath and approached it, my footsteps echoing softly against the pavement. The pull grew stronger, but it wasn't the same overwhelming force that had dragged me into the mirror world before. This was different—gentler, almost welcoming.

When I reached the mirror, I stopped, staring into the glass. My reflection looked back at me, calm and steady, just as it had in the café. There were no distortions, no shadows lurking at the edges. Just me, standing in the alley, the soft glow of twilight framing my silhouette.

But as I stood there, watching myself, something began to shift.

The reflection in the mirror blinked, and for a moment, it wasn't just a reflection anymore. It was **her**—the guide, the version of myself who had led me through the mirror world, the one who had shown me the way forward. She was back, her presence gentle but undeniable, standing in the mirror as though she had always been there.

I didn't flinch this time. I didn't feel the need to run. I simply stared at her, and she stared back, a small, knowing smile playing at the corners of her lips.

"You found me," she said softly, her voice clear and steady, though it seemed to come from inside my own mind as much as from the reflection.

I nodded, my heart beating steadily in my chest. "I didn't think I was looking for you."

She smiled, the kind of smile that felt both sad and hopeful at the same time. "You weren't. But I was waiting."

I took a step closer, my fingers brushing the cool surface of the mirror. "Why now? Why here?"

Her eyes softened, and she looked at me with a kind of tenderness that I hadn't expected. "Because you're ready."

I frowned slightly, not quite understanding. "Ready for what?"

She stepped forward in the reflection, her presence filling the mirror as though she were standing on the other side of a window, just out of reach but close enough to feel. "To let go," she said gently. "To move on."

I stared at her, the weight of her words settling over me like a quiet revelation. "I thought I already had. I thought I'd faced everything."

"You've faced a lot," she agreed, her voice soft. "But there's still one thing left."

I felt a chill run down my spine, not from fear, but from the knowledge that she was right. Even after all the growth, all the acceptance, all the progress I had made, there was still something I had been holding onto. Something I hadn't been ready to let go of.

The mirror world wasn't just about facing the past. It was about learning to live with it, to accept it as part of who I was. But now, standing in this alley, staring at the reflection of myself that had guided me through so much, I realized there was one final step I hadn't taken.

"I'm scared," I whispered, my voice trembling with the weight of the truth.

Her expression softened, and she nodded, understanding. "I know. But you don't have to be."

I closed my eyes for a moment, feeling the cool air of the alley around me, the solid ground beneath my feet. I had been so focused on fixing myself, on finding wholeness, that I hadn't allowed myself to truly let go of the need to control it all. The need to control every piece of my story.

When I opened my eyes again, the reflection was still there, waiting patiently.

"I'm ready," I said softly, the words feeling both like a surrender and a declaration of strength.

The reflection smiled, and for the first time, it felt like I was looking at a friend. A true companion who had been with me all along, waiting for this moment.

"You are," she said simply. "And now, it's time to move forward."

I reached out, my hand resting on the surface of the mirror, and for the briefest moment, I thought I felt her hand on the other side, mirroring mine. The connection between us was undeniable, but as I stood there, I felt the tension in my chest begin to ease.

I wasn't leaving her behind. She was a part of me, and always would be. But I didn't need to hold onto her anymore. I didn't need to hold onto the mirror world or the reflection. I was ready to walk forward on my own.

With a deep breath, I stepped back from the mirror, letting my hand fall to my side. The reflection watched me for a moment longer, her eyes filled with understanding, and then, slowly, she began to fade. The glass shimmered, the light catching on the silver frame, and in an instant, she was gone.

I stood there for a long moment, staring at the empty mirror. It reflected only the alley now, the quiet street behind me, and the soft glow of the setting sun.

It was over.

I smiled to myself, a sense of peace settling over me as I turned away from the mirror and walked back down the alley. The city stretched out before me, the last rays of sunlight casting everything in a warm, golden light. I had faced my reflection, faced the mirror world, and now, I was finally free.

Free to live.

Free to move forward.

Free to be **me**.

Chapter 40: The Door Closed

The sun had dipped below the horizon, leaving behind a warm twilight glow as I made my way back through the quiet streets of the city. The air was cool, the soft hum of the evening settling over everything like a peaceful sigh. As I walked, the world around me seemed to hold its breath, as though waiting for something, though I wasn't sure what.

I had let go of the reflection. The mirror world had released me, its echoes fading into the background of my life. I no longer felt the pull of the shadows or the weight of the past pressing down on me. There was only this moment, this quiet, stillness, and the sense of freedom that came with it.

But as I moved through the familiar streets, something pulled at me once more. Not the same insistent tug of the mirror world, not fear or dread, but a gentle reminder that there was one last thing left to do.

The mirror world had always been a part of my journey, and now that I had stepped away from it, I knew I had to return to the place where it had all begun. One last visit. One final moment of closure.

I turned down the street that led to my apartment, the shadows growing longer as the last light of day faded. The quiet was comforting now, not eerie or foreboding, and I welcomed the stillness as I walked. When I reached my apartment building, I paused at the door, my hand resting on the cool metal of the handle.

This was the door that had led me to everything—the fear, the darkness, the reflection, the revelations. It had been the starting point, the entryway to the mirror world, though I hadn't known it at the time. And now, as I stood there, I realized it would also be the place where the final chapter of this journey would close.

I opened the door and stepped inside.

The apartment was just as I had left it, quiet and still, bathed in the soft glow of the lamps I had turned on before I left. I moved through the space slowly, taking in the familiar surroundings, the furniture, the small details of my life that had once felt like barriers between me and the truth. Now, they felt like home.

But the mirror was still there.

It hung on the wall in the hallway, just as it always had. For a long time, it had been a source of fear and uncertainty, a portal to a world I didn't understand. But now, as I approached it, I felt only peace. I knew what it was, what it had shown me, and I knew that it no longer held any power over me.

I stood in front of the mirror, my reflection looking back at me with calm eyes. There were no shadows, no flickers of movement, no whispers at the edges of my mind. Just me. The person I had fought so hard to become. The person I had always been, but had finally learned to accept.

I reached out and touched the surface of the mirror, my fingers grazing the cool glass. It felt solid, real, and I knew that this was no longer a doorway to the mirror world. The door had closed.

There was no longer any need for it.

I smiled at my reflection, feeling the weight of everything that had happened lift from my shoulders. The mirror had been a tool, a guide, a way for me to see the parts of myself I had been too afraid to confront. But now, it was just a mirror. Just a reflection of who I was in this moment.

I stepped back, letting my hand fall to my side, and for a moment, I simply stood there, taking it all in. The journey, the fear, the pain—it had all led me to this place. To this moment of quiet understanding. I had come through the mirror world, and I had come out the other side, not perfect, but whole in a way that I hadn't thought possible.

I turned away from the mirror and walked into the living room, feeling a sense of closure settle over me like a blanket. The air in the apartment felt different now, lighter, more open. The echoes of the past no longer clung to the walls or hovered in the shadows. They were just memories now, a part of me, but not the whole story.

I sat down on the couch, the quiet hum of the evening filling the space around me. For the first time in a long time, I felt truly at peace. Not because everything was resolved or because I had found all the answers, but because I had learned to live with the questions. I had learned to live with the cracks, the flaws, the parts of myself that would never be fully fixed.

And that was enough.

As I sat there, the light outside the windows fading into the soft darkness of night, I realized that the journey wasn't over. It would never truly be over. There would always be new challenges, new fears, new moments of doubt. But now, I knew how to face them. I knew how to walk through the shadows without losing myself in them.

I stood and moved to the window, looking out at the city below. The lights of the buildings glowed softly in the darkness, each one a reminder that life went on, that the world kept turning no matter what. And I was part of that world now, fully, completely.

As I watched the city, a quiet sense of joy bloomed in my chest. Not the kind of joy that comes from fleeting happiness, but the kind of joy that comes from knowing that I had survived. That I had faced the darkest parts of myself and come through them stronger, more whole.

I turned away from the window, feeling the pull of sleep beginning to settle over me. The day had been long, and I was tired, but it was a good kind of tired. The kind that comes from hard-won peace.

I walked back through the apartment, passing the mirror one last time. My reflection looked back at me, calm, steady, and I smiled at it. The mirror was just a mirror now. It had done its work, and I was ready to move forward.

I turned off the lights, one by one, and made my way to the bedroom. As I lay down, the quiet of the night wrapped around me, and I felt the last remnants of the mirror world fade into the background, like a distant memory that no longer needed to be revisited.

The door to the mirror world had closed.

And I was ready for whatever came next.

Don't miss out!

Visit the website below and you can sign up to receive emails whenever Johnny Gee publishes a new book. There's no charge and no obligation.

https://books2read.com/r/B-A-NXELC-REPBF

BOOKS2READ

Connecting independent readers to independent writers.

Also by Johnny Gee

Cadence of Growth
Cracks In The Silence
Harvest of Secrets: The Hidden Legacy
Locked Away With A Loaded Gun
Raging Rails
The Silent Screams
A Life Intertwined: Charlie's Story
Ashes of the Obsidian Tower
Psychedelic Reverie
Beneath The Watcher's Eye
The Curse of Hollow Creek
The Space Between The Mirror

Milton Keynes UK
Ingram Content Group UK Ltd.
UKHW020754231024
450026UK00001B/26